LUNA

A NOVEL

by Delacorta

Translated by Victoria Reiter

SUMMIT BOOKS   *New York*

COPYRIGHT © 1979 BY ÉDITIONS ROBERT LAFFONT
COPYRIGHT © 1983 BY DANIEL ODIER
ENGLISH LANGUAGE TRANSLATION COPYRIGHT © 1984
BY SUMMIT BOOKS, A DIVISION OF SIMON & SCHUSTER, INC.
ALL RIGHTS RESERVED
INCLUDING THE RIGHT OF REPRODUCTION
IN WHOLE OR IN PART IN ANY FORM
PUBLISHED BY SUMMIT BOOKS
A DIVISION OF SIMON & SCHUSTER, INC.
SIMON & SCHUSTER BUILDING
1230 AVENUE OF THE AMERICAS
NEW YORK, NEW YORK 10020
SUMMIT BOOKS AND COLOPHON ARE TRADEMARKS OF
SIMON & SCHUSTER, INC.
DESIGNED BY DANIEL CHIEL
MANUFACTURED IN THE UNITED STATES OF AMERICA

1 3 5 7 9 8 6 4 2

FIRST AMERICAN EDITION

LIBRARY OF CONGRESS CATALOGING IN PUBLICATION DATA

Odier, Daniel, date.
Luna.

I. Title.
PQ2675.D5L8613   1984   843'.914   83-27192
ISBN 0-671-49379-5

FOR CHUCK. . . . Top of the world, Ma!

CHAPTER

1

ALL OF A SUDDEN WINTER SPLIT and summer sidled in but Alba had not waited for good weather to begin training. She had been jogging regularly for the last two months, her diligence and determination surprising Gorodish.

That morning, sunlight crept across the white sheets to kiss her lightly tanned body. Alba basked in the warmth, stretching like a cat as she ran her fingers through her long blond hair. Her hands closed over her small breasts, checking to see if there had been any change since the night before. For the last few weeks Alba had been rubbing her chest with an African lotion which the magazine ad guaranteed would help develop a large, firm, sexy bosom.

At that very moment, Alba's lithe, feline, well-proportioned young body was starring in Gorodish's dreams as he lay sleeping in the next bedroom.

Paris was still asleep. Gorodish's penthouse lay atop a Left Bank high-rise building. Unseen by the quarter's other early risers, Alba crept from the warm cocoon of her bed, opened the door leading out to the terrace and then, still naked, strolled to the kitchen for her morning glass of banana Nesquik. Carrying the glass outside, she lazed for a while in the cushion-filled rattan lounge chair which was her own contribution to the terrace decor. Gorodish had planted a screen of birch trees around the terrace. The fragile leaves trembled in the early-morning breeze.

Alba took a cold shower, drying herself on a violet bath sheet. The morning was growing warmer now and she decided not to wear a sweat suit. Taking some old jeans from the armoire, Alba cropped the legs high with her nail scissors, and then slipped into what was now a pair of very skimpy shorts. Not bad. She could not run bare-chested through the streets of Paris, so she pulled on a blue T-shirt and left the apartment. Breaking into a run the moment she reached the street, Alba hit her stride almost immediately, moving so fast that she seemed to blur like a background figure in a television commercial. She followed her usual route: down Rue de Beaune, across the Henri IV Bridge to the Right Bank and through the deserted pathways of the Louvre gardens. At the Place de la Concorde, with the Arc de Triomphe looming at the far end of the Champs-Elysées, she slowed and settled into her normal jogging pace. There was no traffic yet and the morning air was clear.

Halfway up the Champs-Elysées she stopped to catch her breath and rest on a bench in front of the Lido Arcade. Alba liked to finish her morning workout with a final sprint up the avenue to the Arc, a small challenge she set for herself at the end of each day's run.

A pearl-gray Lancia coupe came rolling sedately up the avenue. Alba watched as it slowed and came to a stop about six feet away. A handsome young man with black curly hair slithered out of the car and oozed around it toward her. He was fashionably, if conservatively, dressed in a light blue shirt and gray trousers. He seemed very sure of himself.

8

"Hi, there," he said, white teeth flashing. "I'm Steve. Totally awesome morning, isn't it? And here you are, just waiting for me. Has anyone ever told you that you resemble a nymph?"

"The constant nymph," Alba said in a bored voice.

"Howzat?"

"*The Constant Nymph,* by Margaret Kennedy; you can buy it in paperback."

"Oh. Is it good?"

"I don't know; I never read it."

"Ah," said Adonis, taken aback. But he recovered quickly. Another smile. He obviously had great faith in the effect of all those white teeth in the middle of all that tan. "I've had a killer night, hit all the clubs, tooted a few lines of flake, absolute death. Feels good to be outside in the fresh air. What'd you do last night?"

"Went to bed."

"With a boy or a girl?" He eyed Alba with what was evidently his most seductive expression.

"With a crocodile, lots of teeth."

"You're amusing, too. And I'm starving. I've got an idea: why don't we go over to my place, on Avenue Foch, just the other side of the Arc. I'll make breakfast."

"You have any banana Nesquik?"

"No. But I've got some superfine Lapsang souchong tea my mother brought back from London. You'll love it."

"Why don't you come right out and say you want to go to bed with me, instead of talking about tea and your mother?"

Steve sidestepped the question. "I'm not the pushy type, you know? I usually wait until the girl asks for it."

"Before I hop in the sack with a guy," Alba said, "I want to be sure he can deliver. Why don't we play a little game; it's a sort of race. If you win, I'll go to bed with you."

"Sounds okay to me."

"Oh, I know you're going to love it," Alba said with a syr-

9

upy smile. "Why don't we start from here and run all the way to your place?"

"Okay."

Not wanting to alarm him, Alba started off at a slow trot. Steve was confident: after all, he played two hours of tennis every day, and Alba looked more like an angel than an athlete. At first he kept up a running conversation but after a few minutes Alba suggested he save his breath.

They ran side by side in the fragrant morning air, up the Champs-Elysées, past Le Drugstore at the top of the avenue where it met Place de l'Etoile. Steve was breathing hard now. Alba stepped up the pace. He fell behind for a moment, then managed to catch up to her again, sweating and gritting his teeth, his heart pounding as he struggled to keep pace with her. The girl had to be bluffing.

Alba increased the pace again, her legs flashing like a thoroughbred hitting the home stretch. They were running on the grassy median of the Avenue Foch now. Steve's heart felt as if it were going to explode, but he put on one last burst of speed. And collapsed. Not even bothering to look back, Alba ran on, moving easily to the very end of the avenue before disappearing into the morning mist.

As it had every Thursday morning at eight for the last three years, the midnight blue Peugeot 604 sedan pulled up to the curb and Jean-François Delaborde got out. The chauffeur parked the car farther up the street and settled back with a James Bond novel. His boss would be gone exactly one hour, time enough to finish the book.

The office of Dr. Jacques Alcan, France's most famous psychoanalyst, was on the second floor. Delaborde did not wait for the elevator but ran up the stairs, eager to begin his weekly therapy session. For the last three years he had happily shelled out six hundred francs a week in payment for the few, actually the only, moments of perfection in his life.

Delaborde was forty-six. Sole heir to an industrial empire, his work had drained him. Tall and slightly overweight, Delaborde had a babyish, vaguely frightening face, with hair so thick and black it almost looked dyed. Despite the nervous tics that agitated his arms and hands, there was something imposing about the man, yet his physical presence gave no hint of his underlying emotional instability. At times his eyes would glow brightly with a pale fire, an exaltation, a fever that could be kindled by the night, the moon, the sight of certain insects and a particular kind of beauty.

The receptionist, a woman as dignified and bland as a madam in a high-class whorehouse, ushered him directly into Professor Alcan's office. The therapist, a man in his fifties, rose from behind his desk to shake Delaborde's hand. Alcan always made it a point to appear vaguely unhappy as he greeted his patients. That display of tact, along with his precise gestures, infinite attention to detail and circumspect air gave him the look of an undertaker. The room was a perfect reflection of the man: solid mahogany desk, small note pad and pencil, bronze-colored carpeting, walls covered in grass cloth, artfully arranged lighting, large, comfortable couch and an armchair. The few stray motes of sunshine that managed to filter through the tobacco-colored drapes freckled the inner edge of the windowsill.

Jean-François Delaborde hung up his jacket, unbuttoned his vest, loosened his tie, undid his collar button and stretched out on the couch.

He felt wonderful. His mind and body were completely relaxed. At first he had been intimidated by the silence, but now ideas floated freely through his mind.

Alcan seated himself directly behind his patient. Delaborde could feel the man's presence but could see nothing

11

but the wall covered with woven grass cloth, one lighter thread holding the darker fibers together. Delaborde's hand plunged into his trousers' pocket and he began to finger the matchbox containing his favorite scarab.

"I feel comfortable in this office," he began. "In the beginning it was very difficult, leaving here and going back to the real world, but it's easier now. And the good feeling lasts longer now, sometimes the whole week. It's not that I'm any happier, you know? It's just that I've managed to rid myself of all the negative energy that was getting in my way, holding me back. I've reached a sort of . . . neutral state I suppose you'd call it. Lately I've begun to feel that there must be more to life . . . something better. It's as if, as if, everything I ever took for granted, all my ideas of what life is about, are wrong. Sometimes I feel as if I'll never have any more than this . . . dull neutrality. Sometimes I fantasize another kind of life; I mean a completely different kind of life, free of the social restraints I grew up with, free of everything . . . the physical and mental restraints. I know it must sound utopian. . . ."

Alcan knew that his patient was primed and ready. He had been leading him along carefully, subtly, without too obviously pointing him in this direction. Now it was time to reap the harvest of three years' work.

Alcan spoke and Delaborde was surprised at the tone of his voice, less the therapist than a good friend, a sharer of secrets, an affectionate conspirator.

"You've made amazing progress these last three years," Alcan said. "In your last few sessions it's become increasingly apparent to me that you are finally in touch with your deepest self, the deepest roots of your personality. It was predictable that at some point you would want to change your life. I'm not in the least surprised that you have begun to fantasize living out that age-old dream of being totally

12

yourself, of refusing to bow to convention. I can sense that you want to rid yourself of all your old behavior patterns. You're right that on one level it does sound vaguely utopian, but you mustn't forget that throughout history there have been some men of vision who have managed to act out their fantasies. You must keep that in mind when we begin to discuss what your future life might be like. I recently attended a psychoanalytic convention in Osaka, where one of my colleagues presented a paper on the psychology of the missing person. Did you know that there are literally thousands of missing persons in the world, people who simply disappear and are never found again? It's as if they've managed to evaporate into thin air. Fascinating. I've been considering various aspects of the problem for some time now and have come to the conclusion that the very act of disappearing might be useful as . . . well, as the ultimate form of psychoanalytic therapy."

"Interesting," Delaborde said. "I suppose everybody has fantasized leaving the house to buy a pack of cigarettes and never coming back."

"I've also come to the conclusion that only those patients totally in touch with their innermost selves can find happiness in disappearing. The others usually wind up reproducing the same patterns of dissatisfaction in their new environment. However, I am now convinced that you are the perfect candidate for what I call Disappearance Therapy."

"Are you serious?"

"Perfectly. In fact, I've put together a support system for my patients who decide to adventure into this new form of treatment. My network is very efficient in helping organize the disappearance. I trust you appreciate that you are one of the few people to whom I've spoken of this rather advanced form of therapy, and I know you will respect the traditional rule of patient-doctor confidentiality, no matter what decision you finally make. I'm offering you something very simple, really: the chance to live your life as you see fit, free of all social restraint."

"I suppose your organization is, well, only semilegal," Delaborde said slowly. "There must be enormous problems. . . ."

"All men are free to choose their own lives," Alcan said. "There is no law that can force someone to waste his life. Of course, a buffer must be built between the rest of the world and the person who has chosen to disappear. In the normal course of events, this may lead to the commission of certain acts which on the surface might appear illegal but which are perfectly harmless, I assure you."

Delaborde was silent. A succession of mad images raced through his mind as his entire being began to turn outward, focusing on the possibilities of a new life, a new reality: a reality adapted to his deepest, most secret needs. Alcan's voice tore Delaborde from his reverie.

"Take some time to think it over. If you're interested, we'll discuss it in more detail during your next few sessions."

"Of course," Delaborde said as he rose from the couch, buttoned his collar and vest, straightened his tie and put on his jacket. He wrote out a check, placed it on the mahogany desk and left the office.

Surprised at seeing him so soon, the chauffeur laid aside the book he had been reading. He still had thirty pages to go in *For Special Services.*

Alba returned to the apartment, her arms laden with the morning newspapers and fresh croissants. Gorodish had already prepared coffee and set the table on the terrace. Little by little their lives were becoming more organized. Even Alba's escapades now took place within a rather rigid, and at

14

times ascetic, framework of behavior to which Gorodish insisted she adhere.

He sat at the Steinway grand piano Alba had given him, picking his way through a Haydn sonata. Alba let the newspapers fall to the floor and rushed over to kiss him on the neck. Gorodish inhaled her subtle odor, noting, with some surprise, the high-cut shorts, before turning back to the adagio he had been practicing.

"You play that very well," Alba said.

"My own form of exercise."

"I'm really in shape now," Alba said. "I made it all the way to the Bois de Boulogne today. Some idiot tried to pick me up but he couldn't keep up with me. I left him puking on Avenue Foch."

Gorodish smiled as he imagined the scene.

"Sweet, darling Serge," Alba wheedled, "I want to ask you a favor." Gorodish's eyebrows rose and he waited.

"It's about your hair. It's much too short. Won't you let it grow out? Or shave it off, like Kojak?"

"I'll think about it."

"May I dunk my croissant in your coffee?"

Gorodish watched Alba closely. Each day brought new changes in the body and mind of his darling protégée, his shooting star, his comet. A certain satisfaction filled his soul and for a long moment he seemed very far away.

Alcan hated driving through the tunnel at Saint-Cloud on the western outskirts of Paris. He felt as if all the filth in the world accumulated in the tunnel, just waiting for him to drive by in his immaculate white Rolls-Royce. Alcan could have afforded to hire a chauffeur, but he loved driving the Rolls himself. The warm patina of the worn blue leather interior went beautifully with the white, hand-rubbed lacquered body.

15

A quarter of an hour later he maneuvered the classic white Rolls-Royce into his garage and entered the twelve-room house he shared with his two pet iguanas, Freud and Jung. Jung had a skin condition.

Alcan loved his home, he loved the long suite of rooms, the absolute silence behind the barrier of double-glazed windows, the thick Chinese rugs and contemporary Italian furniture.

Alcan walked through the large living room, its bare walls enlivened by a single Mondrian oil painting, through the music room, the library, the study, and into his bedroom. Beyond the bedroom lay a steam room, a Jacuzzi hot tub and the usual standard bathroom fixtures.

Alcan undressed and stepped into the cedar hot tub whose lightly scented water was held at constant body temperature. This was where Alcan came when he was troubled or depressed, or when there were plans to be made. Ideas came more easily to him as he lounged in the swirling water. Alcan knew what Delaborde's answer would be: the man was ready. There was no need to wait before beginning to organize what would be the eighth disappearance of a patient.

The organization was functioning smoothly now. His network of efficient, competent, if somewhat marginal, operatives helped keep the therapy going. Thanks to Alcan, seven businessmen and industrialists were already living out their deepest fantasies. Alcan's fees were in direct proportion to his patients' personal fortunes. In the last two years the psychoanalyst had deposited eleven million dollars in his Swiss bank account, over and above what he had spent providing the ideal setting and life-style for each of his missing patients.

One of the analysands was now living a very simple life, having been adopted into a tribe of Amazon Indians. Another sailed the seven seas, another played at sultan in a

16

small palace in northern India, still another man was a fur trapper in Canada. One patient collected stamps. Another had become the disciple of a Zen master. Of all his patients, Alcan confessed to a certain admiration for the one who had undergone plastic surgery to alter his appearance and now lived next door to his own family, spying on them.

Alcan knew exactly what sort of life Delaborde would choose. But for the first time he found himself facing a difficult problem, one that contained a definite risk to himself.

Stepping from his hot tub, Alcan put on a white silk robe and crawled into his oversized bed. Picking up the telephone, he called one of his associates, a real-estate agent specializing in the sale of luxury homes all over the world.

"Hello, Jerome; this is Jacques. I think I may have a new client for you. Do you have anything? We'll have to move fast on this one."

"What are you looking for?" the real-estate agent asked. "A mogul palace? A beach house in California?"

"No, I think we'll be staying in France this time. We'll need a small château, something rather austere, and isolated, of course. A comfortable place, in move-in condition."

"I can't remember everything on our list. Why don't you let me look through the files? I'm sure I can find something. I'll drop off some brochures at your office. . . ."

"All right. But by tomorrow at the latest."

Delaborde drove up the lane toward his home. His wife had insisted they buy the luxurious house in the suburbs from its original, movie-star owner, but Delaborde hated the place. Everything about it offended him. He despised the vain display, the ostentatious show of luxury that apparently satisfied his wife's tastes and ambitions. The Spanish-style house looked out of place in the heart of the Ile-de-France, the soft countryside surrounding Paris. The garden was par-

17

ticularly atrocious, with its silly, heart-shaped swimming pool, gas tiki torches, pink garden furniture, close-cropped lawn, tennis court and showy barbecue pit, its chimney an insult to good taste. A hideous purple American car stood in the driveway. Delaborde could not bring himself even to think about the inside of the house. Its decor was the result of the combined efforts of his wife and a popular young interior designer who was undoubtedly her lover.

Delaborde was unpleasantly surprised to find a crowd of people fluttering around the swimming pool and lounging around the garden with cocktail glasses in their hands.

His wife came to greet him. She was wearing a light, emerald-green chiffon dress from which her disgustingly tan shoulders and sun-cured face rose in dubious splendor. All their friends thought she was beautiful.

"It's such lovely weather, darling," she said. "I called a few friends to join us for dinner. I'm having tables set up around the pool. Did you have a good day?"

"I'm tired," Delaborde replied; "long staff meeting, some American colleagues arriving tomorrow. You won't be angry with me if I don't join you for dinner?"

"Oh, dear, you have been so gloomy lately," his wife said.

Delaborde kissed her on the forehead and walked around to the far side of the house, hoping to avoid the guests. When he reached his study, he pulled the drapes closed and sat down in his leather easy chair, wondering how his wife could love the sun, much less expose her body to it. His mind drifted as he thought of the alternate future Alcan had offered him. The doctor was right: he was ready to take the plunge. The idea of walking *out*, of disappearing, filled him with joy.

The Rolls-Royce was black, a small extravagance that Gorodish had ordered to please his nymph. The car rolled

18

slowly through the twilight as the lights of Paris began to blaze and great pink slashes of color tinted the sky. Alba had dressed for the occasion. She was wearing a long evening skirt of black lamé, black stockings, black tennis shoes encrusted with sequins and an incredible halter top made of a silver scarf twisted around her neck, crossed over her breasts and knotted in the back. Her belly was a gleaming triangle, revealing the delicate crater of her navel. Her bare shoulders, arms and back glowed in the gathering dark. The driver kept his eyes on the rearview mirror more than on the road.

Alba felt as if the Rolls were skimming along, propelled by the late spring breeze. Gorodish, usually more bohemian in matters of dress, wore a midnight-blue dinner jacket. His left arm lay lightly across Alba's shoulders as she pressed herself against him. They both seemed to be radiating joy, as if determined to enjoy every moment of this gala evening.

They drove through the Place de la Concorde with its lights and fountains, past the pink-tinged facade of the Louvre and up Avenue de l'Opéra. Turning left into Boulevard de la Madeleine, they drove around Place de la Madeleine and into Rue Royale. The Rolls came to a stop in front of Maxim's.

Alba's entrance into the red and gold restaurant was sheer magic. The murmur of voices faded and several dozen pairs of eyes turned in her direction, the men enchanted, the women glaring jealously. All eyes followed the shooting star as she sparkled and glittered her way to a reserved table. The air crackled with fantasies. Champagne. A thousand golden particles blended into the fire that gleamed in Alba's eyes.

Delaborde could not wait until his next session. Impatient and feverish with excitement, he pushed his way into Alcan's office on the heels of the afternoon's last patient.

19

Alcan had been expecting him. Real-estate folders lay waiting on his desk.

Alcan handed Delaborde the files from his desk. "If none of these suits you, we can find something else."

Delaborde pulled out the photographs, spread them across Alcan's desk and examined them closely. It took him only two minutes to make his choice. It was a very beautiful small château. Aerial photographs showed the surrounding forest, and other pictures displayed various angles of the building, including the interior, a pure marvel of perfectly restored thirteenth-century architecture. The file included a building inspector's report, a general description of the château and its environs, a ground plan, an inventory of the furniture and furnishings. The château was located in the middle of seventy acres of fenced-in land. The main building was ready for him to move in. The price seemed reasonable: only two million, three hundred thousand francs.

"It's a dream," Delaborde said. "And it's isolated, isn't it? Exactly what I wanted." He smiled, exposing long, slightly pointed teeth.

"Do you want any remodeling done before you move in?"

"Yes, but nothing major. The main thing will be to redo the attic. According to the blueprints it seems to have been used as a library. I'll want a large skylight cut into the roof so that the entire room is bathed in moonlight. And I'll need an electronic security system. There are a few other minor changes, but I can take care of them once I've moved in."

"Fine. Then I'll have the real-estate agent draw up a bill of sale. Now, for the most important part: your change of identity. I'll give you the address of a man who does that sort of work; he'll make you a new passport, driver's license, credit cards and so forth. Could you go see him tonight? He's waiting for you."

20

Delaborde was feverish with excitement. The idea of being anonymous, and more than slightly outside the law, was very stimulating.

"Are you sure you're ready to do this?" Alcan asked. "You'll have to live completely removed from the world. You won't be able to leave the château: it will be too dangerous to appear in public."

"I'm sick of my life," Delaborde said. "I'll be only too happy to give up all that nonsense. But there is one thing I must have in order to be completely happy. You know what I'm talking about. . . ."

Delaborde leaned back in the chair. His eyes darkened and began to gleam as he described in detail the image of his desires.

The mirrors in Maxim's reflected Alba's image in waves of infinity. Never in her life had she tasted so many varied and subtle flavors. When they finally rose from the table Gorodish saw that several of the other diners had been waiting for that moment. The entire restaurant watched as Alba, her eyes vague and dreamy, crossed the room with her lithe, swinging stride.

Back safely in the Rolls, Gorodish announced that he intended to show his nymph the cathedral at Chartres. The Rolls drove up the Champs-Elysées, through the Bois de Boulogne and out the western *autoroute*, purring along at a steady hundred miles per hour.

Gorodish touched Alba's hair, her face; he ran his hand down her long slender neck. Alba stretched like a cat and her slim fingers crept into Gorodish's heavier, warmer palm. She slid his hand under the scarf and pressed it against her left breast. In a hoarse whisper she said, "Don't you think my breasts are bigger?"

Alba's forehead furrowed anxiously as she waited for his

reply. Gorodish smiled. "I was just going to mention it," he said.

"Why are we going to see some old cathedral? We could go home instead and make love."

A shiver ran through Gorodish's body. Tenderly, he whispered, "I think we'll wait until there are a few more candles on your birthday cake. . . ." Alba was obviously hurt. The lights of the Saint-Cloud tunnel flashed orange on her face, revealing two large tears at the rim of her lower lashes. The tears welled up and ran down her cheeks onto her neck. Gorodish placed his lips against her throat and licked the salt from her skin.

Delaborde crossed the courtyard of a building in the heart of Montparnasse and rang the bell next to a brightly painted blue door. Moments later he heard footsteps and sensed someone behind the door. A small peephole opened and then closed again. Several locks clicked and the door swung open. The man standing in the doorway looked more like an artist than a forger. But after all, Delaborde thought, forgers are artists, aren't they?

The man's face was as sharp as a knife. His eyes were enormous and dark, and a tuft of messy hair sprang over his forehead. His back was hunched, as if he had spent his life bending over official documents.

"Professor Alcan sent me."

"I've been expecting you. Come in."

They climbed up to the second floor, crossed a large room filled with disorderly piles of dusty art books and magazines stacked high between dilapidated chairs, then went up a spiral staircase to the next floor and entered an artist's studio.

The artist was obviously a member of the photorealist school of painting. He seemed to have a penchant for reproducing supermarket shelves. Another series of oils depicted

22

women reading magazines, the text and photographs rendered in excruciatingly lifelike detail.

The painter watched as Delaborde examined his work. His usual clients were rarely interested in aesthetics.

"You appreciate art," he said, his icy reserve melting slightly.

"Yes. I like your work. . . ."

"Thank you. Would you please sit down here?"

Delaborde noticed the stool and the portrait camera. The painter switched on two strobes. "Look this way. Lift your head a little. That's perfect." The strobes flashed twice.

"That's it. Your papers will be ready tomorrow. Have you decided on a name?"

"I thought I'd call myself Louis Garrard."

"All right. And your profession?"

"Chief executive officer."

"Yes, that's vague enough."

Delaborde rose and began examining the paintings again. A crazy idea had just occurred to him.

"Have you ever accepted a commission?" he asked.

"You mean for a painting?" the artist said in a slightly warmer voice.

"Yes."

"I have once or twice. But I need a subject that truly inspires me. You know how it is: I spend so much time forging papers that I prefer to keep my personal work as pure and free of outside influences as possible. I would need to feel some real enthusiasm for the subject. . . ."

"I've been thinking about a particular kind of painting, a moonlit landscape," Delaborde said. "I don't know exactly how to describe it. . . . Well, anyway, if the idea interests you at all, I'll pay your travel and living expenses. I can afford to be fairly generous. If you decide not to take the commission, I'll pay your per diem expenses anyway. But if you do decide to take the commission, I'll make it worth your while. Why don't you think it over for a week or two and then, once I've settled in, I'll send you my new address. If you like, you can come see me."

"All right. I'll bring my paints and brushes just in case. Now, can you come back here tomorrow, around four?"

"Of course. I hesitate to bring this up, but are you certain these identity papers will pass inspection?"

"I've had clients from all around the world, and not one of them has ever had reason to complain. You'll be a little nervous at first, especially crossing borders and so on, but you'll get used to it."

"I'll be staying in France."

"Then there's no problem. My work has even fooled the sophisticated electronic systems they use in the United States. Don't worry: I'm the best in the business."

Reassured, Delaborde left, for the first time in years happy to be going home. In a few weeks he would no longer have to look at the same old faces, faces for which he no longer felt anything but indifference. Except, perhaps, for his oldest daughter. Occasionally he did feel a twinge of affection for her.

It was six in the morning when the Rolls deposited Gorodish and Alba at their apartment building on Rue de l'Université. The sky was a deep, vivid blue and a few stars still twinkled far above the horizon. Suddenly, Alba said, "Come on, let's go to Place Saint-Sulpice."

They walked up Rue Bonaparte and into the large square. "You go sit down on one of those little pillars," Alba ordered.

Obediently, Gorodish sat down, facing the fountain in the middle of the deserted square.

Alba went directly to the fountain, unknotting the silver

scarf covering her breasts and letting it fall to the cobblestones. She slipped off her skirt, kicked off her shoes and appeared half naked in the violet light, wearing nothing but her stockings, black satin panties and a black satin garter belt. Astonished, enchanted, Gorodish hastily looked around the square, making sure that there were no other witnesses to the strange and marvelous scene. A taxi drove by and disappeared. To his left he could see the lights of the police station. Nothing moved.

Alba climbed up into the fountain, moving with all the grace of a mermaid. She patted the lion-head spigots and then clambered up into the top basin. Letting herself glide forward into the water, she emerged from the waves, a dripping, golden-haired goddess. Then, her arms swinging, her laughter filling the square, Alba marched around the basin before turning to face Gorodish, her legs spread wide, her hands on her breasts, an indescribable smile on her face. Bewitched, entranced, Gorodish looked up at her for several long moments. Then he rose and walked toward the fountain, stooping to retrieve the silver scarf, skirt and shoes which lay on the cobblestones. Alba climbed down from the fountain, floating toward Gorodish, moving toward him like a character in a Jean Cocteau film. She embraced him, drying her body against his dinner jacket. Gorodish handed her the skirt, her shoes, the filmy scarf. It clung to her damp skin, underlining the fragile sensuality of her young breasts as she stood shivering in the cool dawn air.

CHAPTER

2

THE LAST HOUR OF ALBA'S DAILY lesson was over. Her tutors had all been chosen on the basis of Gorodish's own personal theories of education; his choices matched Alba's temperament perfectly. Her tutors were all young and passionately interested in their subjects; the work periods were short but intense. Alba had had no trouble passing the state examinations for pupils who studied at home. Besides the usual subjects, Gorodish saw to it that his angel studied art history, music, classical Indian dance and photography.

After having discussed the works of de Maupassant for an hour with Gustave, her literature teacher, Alba ended the study period by offering the tutor a Coke. Gustave politely declined the offer and, before leaving, suggested that on his next visit they discuss *Red Harvest*, by Dashiell Hammett.

Gorodish had decided to initiate Alba into the delights of Viennese pastry by preparing a Sacher torte. He was in the kitchen, wrestling with a food processor, a blender and several other utensils designed to make the cook's work easier.

Alba wanted to go for a walk. She had been planning to buy Gorodish a small gift, perhaps a recording of classical music. It was time she put her newly acquired knowledge of music to use.

Alba showered and went through her closet, looking for something to suit her mood. She put on a two-tone silver and violet chintz anorak. Its iridescent stripes, matched to the tight, pearl-gray capri pants, made her shine like an old-fashioned candy box. She slid on a gold-tone bracelet and for a finishing touch, slipped into a pair of Indian sandals. Opening the lacquered box in which she kept her money, Alba took several ten-franc notes and stuffed them into her pants pocket.

Before leaving, she went into the kitchen to kiss Gorodish good-bye, winking broadly as she made her exit. She looked so beautiful that Gorodish stopped beating his egg whites for a moment just to stare at her.

This was the big day. The château was ready; all the remodeling work had been done. Delaborde was to meet Ludovic, the butler, in a parking area off the A-16 *autoroute*. Ludovic would be driving a Renault 16.

Delaborde had stayed home from the office on the pretext of wanting to work without being interrupted. He strolled through the horrible house one last time as he waited impatiently for the hour of his departure. Two of his daughters were playing tennis; his wife was swimming in the silly pool. Delaborde was tempted to take a few mementos with him: a photograph of his parents, an American entomological encyclopedia, a few articles of clothing in which he felt particularly comfortable. But Alcan's instructions had been explicit: he was to take nothing with him that might give the game away. He would be leaving the past behind; he would be building an entirely new future.

The chauffeur had been given the day off. Now, as he sat

27

on his bed for the last time, Delaborde took out the new identity card and examined it closely. A masterpiece. There was a noise in the living room and he hurriedly put the card away. At the very last moment he decided to change into older, more comfortable clothing. Alcan had helped Delaborde through the last-minute moments of anxiety that had begun to nag him. Now, as he changed his clothing, an almost adolescent excitement gripped him.

Delaborde walked out of the house and toward the pool. Surprisingly, now that the moment to leave had come, he didn't even hate his wife anymore; he could remember the good times they had shared.

"Don't you want to come in for a swim, darling?" she called.

"I'll be back in a little while," he answered. "I'm just going to buy some cigars." She responded with a wave of her hand.

Delaborde got into his car, started the motor and drove past the tennis court for one last look at his children. It suddenly occurred to him that he loved them. He pressed his foot firmly on the gas pedal. This was not the moment to turn sentimental.

A black iron gate barred the dirt driveway running through the thick forest.

"Is this where the property begins?" Delaborde asked, trying to keep his voice steady.

"Yes," Ludovic answered and stopped the car. Taking a key from among several hanging on a large ring, he opened the heavy gate.

Ludovic was tall and looked about forty years old. Smiling and amiable, his appearance was deceptive. The Yugoslav had been involved in shady deals his entire life. He had fought as a mercenary for ten years and, inevitably, had

28

wound up in the drug trade. At one time he had had dreams of going straight and had found a job as a butler with a family of aristocrats. That was where he had met Alcan.

Ludovic relocked the gate behind them and they drove on. The château was invisible from the entrance to the property. Delaborde felt as if the woods were closing in on him, growing as thick and threatening as a jungle in a painting by Rousseau.

They drove into an open area and the pure, gray shape of the château appeared before them. A large tower, topped by a pyramidal roof, loomed high over the building's two wings. One ell was massive and rectangular in shape; the other was longer and more graceful.

The château was sublime. Built of grisaille and slate, its clean lines were in perfect proportion to the site on which it stood. A paved courtyard lay in front of the building. The shutters, painted a tasteful light gray, blended with the natural color of the stone.

Delaborde shivered with happiness when he saw the large skylight set into the high attic roof.

"Would you like a tour of the property before dinner?" Ludovic asked.

"Yes, absolutely. Show me everything."

Charley had been Alcan's patient for two years before putting an end to the therapy. Charley was a gigolo and, at a very young age, had understood the profit to be made with his good looks. Charley had had a series of rich "protectors" and had never wanted for money. He had lived in the great hotels of the Côte d'Azur, or in sumptuous apartments in Paris, his life leaving him little time for the development of his true talent as a dress designer. That life had lasted until the unhappy day a rival had left his mark on Charley's beautiful face. Now, a wide scar ran from the corner of his

29

right eye, across his cheek, and down to his ear. Charley had fallen on hard times in the protégé business and during the course of his analysis had come to the conclusion that there had to be a better way to make a living. Alcan introduced Charley to several of his acquaintances, and the boy spent a few months working as a chauffeur. But his soul had been so ravaged and luxury had so corrupted him that he quickly turned to pimping for other young men, introducing them to people he met through Alcan.

From the very beginning, Alcan had had Charley in mind for the Delaborde disappearance. The doctor had chosen wisely: a chance to make some easy money and the illegality surrounding the project had appealed to Charley immediately. Alcan had always had a taste for the vulgar, especially when it was camouflaged under a certain social polish. Charley was perfect.

The boy had turned capricious just before he was to leave for the château, insisting that he absolutely had to have some new shirts. Alcan decided to indulge him and sent Ludovic to drive Delaborde to his new home. Alcan knew that Charley's absolute contempt for women would be an asset in carrying out the last phase of the project, the part that would guarantee Delaborde's happiness as the latest subject of Disappearance Therapy.

The white Rolls-Royce moved slowly up the Champs-Elysées. Charley stared out at the stores, window-shopping. Suddenly he told Alcan to stop. "Here we are," Charley said. "The Lido Arcade. You can always find something not too tacky here."

"There's no place to park," Alcan said.

"Well, you'll just have to double-park. The cops aren't going to bother with a car like yours: they'd be too worried some banker or politician would complain."

Alcan smiled and turned on the blinking emergency lights. He left the motor running.

30

                          *   *   *

Charley tried on a dozen different shirts, blatantly showing off his long-muscled, lightly tanned body to the admir-
ing eyes of two giggling salesgirls. Alcan watched the scene
and silently developed a theory on the inherent bad judg-
ment of the young.

Charley finally chose four shirts and a pair of expensive
moccasins. Alcan paid for them and asked for a receipt. He
would charge the purchases to Delaborde's account.

Alba caught sight of the white Rolls-Royce and stopped
dead in her tracks. It was even more beautiful than the black
Rolls Gorodish had rented for their gala evening. The sweet
hum of its engine drew her forward, an idea growing within
her as naturally as breathing: she would steal the Rolls, drive
it around Paris for a while just to get the feel of it, then pick
up Gorodish and take him for a ride. She could imagine his
surprise.

Alba looked around. Nobody seemed to be watching. Her
heart pounding, she casually walked around the car, opened
the heavy door and slid behind the wheel.

It was immediately obvious to her that a Rolls was far
more complicated to drive than the simple Peugeot 504 she
was used to. Everything seemed to be automatic or power-
assisted, and she could not figure out how the gearshift
worked. Alba decided to approach the problem in a logical,
scientific manner, methodically trying one lever after another. At some point, the Rolls would have to move.

Charley spotted Alba in the Rolls. "Look, boss, do you
see what I see?"

Alcan nodded frantically. The gods seemed to be with
him. "She looks perfect," he said nervously, "but it's too
dangerous, Charley. Not here, not on the Champs-Elysées."

"Don't be silly," Charley said coolly, "this is just the

                              31

place. You take a taxi back to your place and I'll check out the girl. If she fits the bill, I'll bring her to you. If not, I'll drop her off at her home and we'll find someone else."

"All right, all right," Alcan whispered, "but be careful. And give me enough time to get back home and open the garage door."

Charley moved toward the car, taking his time like a real gentleman. Alba was busy pushing buttons and pulling levers. She did not catch sight of Charley until he opened the car door. Then her heart bounded up into her throat and soared off into space. It took her a second or two to realize that the owner of the Rolls was smiling; he did not look as if he was going to call a cop. Alba took a deep breath. Charley slid in, closed the door and lit up a Chesterfield. Alba thought that rich people certainly were strange. She looked at his face and decided that he was probably a movie actor.

"Do you know how to drive?" Charley asked.

"No. I just wanted to sit in it for a while, see what it felt like," Alba said carefully.

"Do you like it?"

"Yeah, uh-huh, it's okay, I guess," Alba said, her smile as naive as she could make it.

"I like it when someone goes with the flow," Charley said. "Most people are so tight-ass about private property they'd never dare get into a car without an engraved invitation."

Alba looked more closely at Charley and suddenly panic filled her.

"Let's go for a ride," Charley said. Alba shook her head, unable to speak. "Oh, yes," Charley said. "Tell me your name and I'll even show you where I live."

The Rolls moved up a wide boulevard and turned into a small, quiet street. Charley drove the car directly into the open garage.

32

"I have to call home," Alba said, sliding out of the Rolls.

"No problem," Charley said, taking her by the arm. "I'll show you where the phone is."

He pushed her into the large white living room. Alcan, seated in a chair, stared at her intently. Instinctively, she recoiled. Charley closed the door. Alba felt trapped and, without stopping to think, turned and tried to run. She saw a flash of Charley's cold face just as he grabbed her and brutally punched her in the stomach.

Alba fell to the carpet, trying desperately to breathe, unable even to cry out. Charley grabbed her hair, dragged her to her knees and pushed her toward Alcan. She fell at the doctor's feet, her face blue from lack of oxygen. Slowly, her breathing became normal again.

"If you say one word I'll hit you again," Charley said, a vicious smile on his face.

Alcan felt a bit uneasy; he loathed violence.

"Easy, Charley; I'm sure this lovely young lady will behave herself. She seems absolutely charming."

Trembling, Alba managed to take a deep breath and pulled herself up into a chair. She could not bring herself to look at Charley. And she thought of Gorodish.

"Do sit here," Alcan said, "facing me. Charley, bring her a glass of water. You didn't have any trouble did you?"

"No problem. The asshole thought Prince Charming had showed up on his white charger."

"Perfect, perfect," Alcan said, rubbing his hands.

Dazed, Alba watched him, realizing that she had just been kidnapped.

"It will do you absolutely no good to scream," Alcan said, looking her over. "Nobody will hear you."

Charley returned carrying a glass of water. His face impassive, he handed it to Alba.

She took two long swallows and then put the glass down. She still had not uttered a word.

"What's her name?" Alcan said.

"Alba," Charley answered.

"What a nice name. Very symbolic."

Alcan opened a small humidor made of thuya burl, the aromatic North African wood, and took out a Rey del Mundo cigar. Squeezing it lightly between two fingers to make sure it was not dry, he lit it.

"What do you want, you crazy old . . ." Alba managed to say.

"It talks," Charley said sarcastically.

"What does your father do?" Alcan demanded.

"Go fuck yourself."

Charley took one step forward. Alcan repeated the question.

"He's a mechanic," Alba said, hate in her voice.

"Well, well, what we've got here is a little working-class dolly trying to pass herself off as a prep-school twat. Amusing, isn't it?" Alcan was relieved. The girl's disappearance would cause less fuss than if she had come from an influential family.

"How old are you?"

"A hundred and two. What's it to you?"

"Really? I would have said fifteen or sixteen."

Alba's mind was working again. One thing was certain: she did not dare say one word about Gorodish.

"What do you want?" Alba said, suddenly seeming more fragile, more desperate.

"Nothing, just yet. It will all be explained to you in good time."

"We'd better get out of here," Charley said.

"You're right."

Alcan disappeared for a moment, then returned holding a hypodermic syringe. Alba saw a few drops of liquid squirt from the needle.

Charley did not give her a chance to scream but covered

34

her mouth with one hand and held her down with the other. Alba struggled so furiously that Alcan was forced to set down the needle and help Charley immobilize her before he could inject her with his own private mixture of tranquilizers.

Alba went limp as the drug hit her. A wave of heat spread through her body and she felt herself slipping into unconsciousness.

Alcan could not resist opening Alba's anorak and inspecting his prize. "A beautiful piece of merchandise," he said. "Delaborde will be ecstatic. We got lucky, Charley. It could have taken us a long time to find something this perfect. It's incredible, isn't it? These days there's absolutely no difference between middle-class and working-class girls. They all dress as if they were born with money and taste."

"She's a pretentious little cunt," Charley said. "You should have seen it: like a greedy jaybird with a piece of shiny junk."

"Are you sure nobody saw you?"

"Positive."

"Okay, then: we're leaving. Carry her out to the car."

"Let's play it safe and put her in the trunk."

"It's too dangerous. She won't be able to breathe."

"Didn't you used to have those dog carriers?"

"That's an idea."

"I'll tie her up, just in case the shot doesn't hold her. . . ."

"I think I have a straitjacket somewhere," Alcan said, going to look for it.

They carried Alba to the car, wrapped her in a blanket and shoved her into the Rolls's large trunk on top of some pillows.

This time his nymph was carrying things too far. It was almost nine o'clock and she had promised to be home early. Gorodish decided it was time he got tough with her again.

Trying to control his temper, he sat down at the Steinway, fingered through a pile of music and then placed the score of Mendelssohn's *Songs Without Words* on the piano stand. He began to play the first Romance in E major.

The white Rolls sped across the province of Berry. Alcan sat hunched and tense in the front seat. This was the first time he had actually taken part in one of the disappearances he had planned.

"I'm counting on you, Charley," Alcan said. "I expect you to keep an eye on everything that goes on in the château. Delaborde's going to be so hysterical he might get out of hand. Ludovic's okay for muscle, but he's not all that bright. I've given orders that the telephone is to be kept under lock and key, but the real danger could come from outside. I want you to do all the shopping, and you'll have to see to it that no strangers come inside the grounds. As far as the girl is concerned, you'll have to judge how she reacts to the situation. Remember, never let your guard down. She must never know where she is, so make sure there's nothing that might reveal the location of the château. You know how these things happen: it's fairly easy in the beginning but after a while people tend to relax and things go wrong."

"I'll keep my eyes open," Charley said, staring at the road.

"Yes, but don't forget we're not in India. With that phony maharajah we set up, the girls were all volunteers and there was absolutely no risk, except that someone might discover that the disappearance had been planned. But it's completely different with Delaborde. It could be very dangerous."

"How much money is there in the bank account?"

"There's enough there to keep this thing going for several years."

"You'll have to find someone to take my place, once everything's working smoothly," Charley said.

"Don't worry. You know you're the only one I trust to set this up."

"What'll we do with the girl, if she doesn't cooperate?"

"We'll sell her to the maharajah," Alcan said. "She'll still be fresh enough for his tastes."

Charley and Alcan drove on in silence, in a hurry to reach the château.

Delaborde walked past the armor-plated door into the small control room housing the alarm system. If one of the infrared cameras detected someone on the grounds, or if someone climbed the fence surrounding the property, or came in over the gate, red lights would flash in every room of the château and an alarm would begin to ring. The intruder would be under the surveillance of six television cameras, his image visible on six television screens in the security room. The alarm would also automatically open the kennel doors where two attack dogs spent their days pacing back and forth.

"Wonderful," Delaborde said.

"It works perfectly," Ludovic said. "We tested it."

"Have the things I ordered arrived?"

"Yes. Did you want to open the packages? They're in the butler's pantry."

"No. I just wanted to be sure everything was here."

At that moment the telephone rang. Ludovic answered it.

"Monsieur Garrard, please."

"May I tell him who is calling?"

"Charley."

Ludovic handed Delaborde the receiver.

"We've got her," Charley said. "We're on our way."

"So soon?" Delaborde gasped.

37

"We got lucky."

"Wonderful! I can't wait to see her. When will you be here?"

"Around four in the morning. Please ask Ludovic to prepare something for us to eat; we won't be stopping on the way."

"Oh, of course. And I can't wait to see you."

It was three in the morning and Gorodish was livid. His anger with Alba had changed into fear, and the pain was visible on his face. For the hundredth time he leaned over the low terrace wall, searching the street. Each time he heard the elevator his hopes rose, only to be dashed again.

Something had happened to her. He tried to tell himself that he had to wait, that she would call, that she was all right.

Gorodish drank the last drop of coffee in the thermos. He sat in the deep silence of the night, his hand resting on the telephone. The windows were open and every ounce of his attention was fixed on the street outside, waiting for the sound of her step.

In desperation he thought of telephoning the police, of seeking their assurance that Alba had not been hurt in a traffic accident, that she was still alive. But Gorodish was cut off from any recourse to the usual legal agencies, cut off from any normal sort of help. He was doomed to wait alone, to act alone, to assume responsibility for the outlaw life he had chosen to live.

The sky seemed a little lighter now; the room began to shed its gloom. Gorodish brewed another pot of coffee and refilled the thermos.

Morning sounds began to fill the city, the noise irritating him and increasing his anxiety. For a moment he thought of calling in a private investigator, then rejected the idea.

What could a private investigator do without clues? Goro-dish looked at his watch. It was five-twenty in the morning. The papers did not come out until eight and he would have to go downstairs to buy them. He did not want to leave the apartment.

As the sun rose higher in the sky, and the city awoke, his hopes of seeing Alba faded.

CHAPTER

3

THERE WAS A BLACK CRATER. Then hundreds of red figures began sliding down, disappearing into the black pit. Alba started up, her body shuddering. There seemed to be something, a large mirror in a gilded frame, and a bed, she was on a bed, sinking into it. She remembered and lay still, tense, listening, not moving, not daring to look around. When at last she was sure she was alone, she lifted up on one elbow and examined her surroundings.

The room was large and square, its decor austere and beautiful, with two barred windows opening out onto the day. The drapes were bluish-green, and there was an armchair covered in the same material. A long table, a chair, a dark wood armoire. Only one lamp was lit. The walls were covered with a honey-colored material and three wood-framed engravings hung on one wall.

Alba could sense that she was far from Paris. She sat up on the bed and discovered that she was still wearing the same clothes. The records she had bought were on the table. She got out of bed. A thick rug on the parquet floor muffled her footsteps as Alba walked over to the window and looked out at the thick forest. The white Rolls and a Renault 16 were parked in the courtyard. A beaten path led into the woods. The other window looked out on a broad slate roof. There were two doors in the room: one led to the bathroom; the second was locked.

Alba tried to think but her mind seemed to be drowning in molasses. Her ideas were fuzzy. She could hear someone talking, far off. Then silence fell again.

Gorodish had fallen into an uneasy sleep. Now he woke, rose from his chair and walked through the apartment into Alba's room, as if expecting to find her asleep in her bed. The bedspread had not been touched. Besides the normal disorder, the only trace left of Alba was a light perfume that hung in the air, an aroma only Gorodish could sense.

Lights were going off in his head and a great emptiness was growing inside him, a painful emptiness that spread through his body until nothing else existed.

He was sure now: everything that he had imagined, everything that he had feared, had happened. A succession of sordid images overwhelmed him. He noticed Alba's purse on the table and opened it, remembering that she had not been carrying anything when she left. All her identification papers were there; there was no way the police could identify her if she was hurt or in an accident. But Gorodish feared something worse. He tried telling himself that he had to do something, to move, but he was lost: he did not know how or where to begin.

Gorodish drank another cup of coffee, took a shower and dressed. He was afraid to leave the apartment, his one remaining link to Alba. He knew she would telephone him if

41

she could. Suddenly he had an idea: he would go to an audio discount store and buy an answering machine.

In an effort to shake himself awake, Gorodish ran down the stairs to the ground floor and hailed a taxi on Boulevard Saint-Germain. Twenty minutes later he was back in the apartment and installing the answering device. Now he was free to move around the city. He tried to imagine what Alba had done after leaving the apartment. Gorodish knew that she often went for a walk on the Champs-Elysées. It was one chance in a million, but it had been his first, intuitive reaction and he had to take it.

Reaching the Lido Arcade, Gorodish entered Lido-Musique and went downstairs into the classical record department. He knew that Alba often came here to shoplift, but he had to try everything. The salesman who resembled a big sad dog was there. Gorodish pretended to interest himself in the records while planning how best to approach the man. It would probably be better if he bought something. He picked up a copy of Bach's English Suites, played by Glenn Gould, and went over to the salesman.

"Pardon me," Gorodish said, "but will I be able to exchange this album?"

"As long as it hasn't been opened. Is it a gift for someone?"

"Yes, well, actually, it's for me. I suppose I better explain: my daughter often buys records here, and she always buys me an album for my birthday. So if by any chance she's already bought this album ... she knows I like Glenn Gould."

"What does she look like?"

"She's thirteen, blond, very pretty."

"Oh, certainly, I know her. I mean, I think I know her. Does she always dress in bright colors?"

"Yes. Recently she's been wearing an outfit of blue and shiny pearl-gray stripes."

42

"Yes, I know the girl. She was here yesterday. I'm surprised to see someone who looks so . . . contemporary, shall we say, buying the Haydn piano sonatas. . . . Oh, maybe I shouldn't have told you, but . . ."

"That's all right."

Gorodish paid for the album and walked out of the store. He had not learned very much, other than that Alba had been on the Champs-Elysées. Something told him that the trouble had started here. But, then, all sorts of trouble inevitably started on the Champs-Elysées.

Discouraged, Gorodish sat down on a bench. A pigeon was bathing in the gutter. Gorodish watched it for a long time, paying no attention to the bum lounging next to him on the bench.

Alcan had a sense of theater and refused to let Delaborde see Alba before she awakened. He had netted a real beauty for his patient and was absolutely determined that the first impression be as strong as possible.

"She must be up by now."

"Should I get her?" Charley asked.

"No," Alcan said, "you frighten her too much, and I want her to be as relaxed as possible. Ludovic, you go get her."

Alba heard steps approaching. She sat up on the bed, staring at the door in terror. A key turned in the lock and Ludovic appeared.

"Good morning, mademoiselle."

Alba was so relieved it was not Charley that she said, "Good morning."

"They're all waiting for you in the living room. If you'd be good enough to follow me . . ."

Alcan and Delaborde had asked Charley to leave them alone with Alba, at least for this first meeting. The moment she saw Alcan, Alba began to back away.

43

"Don't be afraid," Alcan said.

Slowly she came forward into the living room, trying to read her future in Delaborde's smiling face.

"Sit down, Alba," Delaborde said.

She obeyed.

There was a long silence. Delaborde was looking at her in a kindly manner. For the moment he did not seem particularly dangerous.

"Incredible," he said at last. "Beyond my wildest expectations."

"You're satisfied, then?" Alcan asked.

"Absolutely."

"Good. In that case, I leave you to your pleasure. I must be getting back to Paris."

Delaborde accompanied Alcan to the door. Alba heard the Rolls drive away, then Delaborde came back into the living room.

"You must be wondering what this is all about," he said in a friendly manner.

The urge to hit him made her arm jerk, but she restrained herself, thinking it more prudent to wait, especially since he seemed to be in charge now, and he seemed friendly enough.

"If you were kidnapped in the middle of Paris, I think you'd have some questions, too."

"Naturally. But I never tried to steal a car."

"I just wanted to see what the inside looked like."

"Of course. But let us say that it's only fair that you pay for your untoward curiosity one way or another."

A rush of fury rose through her, but she tried not to show her feelings. "Don't you think it's even more *untoward* to kidnap a minor?"

"We're not here to discuss comparative morality," Delaborde said, "but rather to try to come to some sort of agreement. Let us agree that you have been brought here to pay a

44

debt, and that it might take some time before your accounts are settled. It all depends on you."

"How much time?"

"A few months, if you cooperate."

"And afterward?"

"Afterward? Why, you will go home. One thing must be understood: whether or not your time here is pleasant depends on you. Since I, personally, consider your presence here a precious gift, you will be remunerated accordingly. When you leave us, you will have a nice little sum of money. . . ."

Alba began to wonder if she was dealing with a nut case.

"You will have to follow the rules," Delaborde continued. "For instance, we cannot let you go if you know where you've been, so any attempt to discover where we are holding you will have an unhappy effect on your future. You are free to come and go inside the château as you please, and I will be happy to provide you with whatever you need to make your stay here comfortable. Please don't hesitate to ask for anything you want. The most important thing is that you absolutely not try to escape. The château is protected by an electronic surveillance system. It is impossible to escape and extremely dangerous to try. There are two rather ferocious attack dogs on the premises. You will be shown the areas which are open to you. If you go beyond those limits the dogs will automatically be set loose. We will not be able to control them; they have been trained to kill since they were puppies. Besides the dogs, we have two people working here. You know Charley already, and . . ."

"He's crazy," Alba said. "You're not going to leave me alone with him!"

"I'll make sure he doesn't bother you. But one of his duties here is to keep an eye on you. You've also met Ludovic, I believe? The man who brought you downstairs?"

"He's okay, but that Charley . . ."

45

"You will simply have to get used to him. And I must tell you that if you try anything . . . naughty . . . I won't be able to stop him from . . . disciplining you."

"I see," Alba said. "May I call home? I could say that I ran away or something."

"I don't think so. At least, not for the moment. . . ."

"Do I have to stay in my room?"

"No. You're perfectly free to move around."

"Outside, too?"

"Yes. Charley will show you the limits of your territory. And you will remember my warning?"

"I'd like to look around the château," Alba said.

"One last thing: your name is very pretty, but it does not quite serve my purpose. I'd prefer to call you Luna."

"If it makes you happy," Alba said indifferently.

"Are you hungry?"

"No."

"We'll be lunching at one o'clock. I'll see you then, Luna."

"What's your name?"

"Louis."

"Not very original," Alba sniffed. She was beginning to regain her spirits.

"Give me another name, if you like. . . ."

"I'll think about it. Listen, you haven't told me what you brought me here for. . . ."

She could sense Delaborde's embarrassment. "We'll talk about it another time," he said. "Now you may go for your walk."

"Okay. See you later."

Alba went back up to her room. She took a shower and decided to think about the situation. She would tour the château and garden later.

* * *

The bum had been staring at Gorodish for a long time. "You like pigeons, Mac?"

"Pigeons. . . ."

"I like pigeons, and you was watching 'em, so I thought . . ."

"I was thinking about something else."

"There's moments like that in everybody's life," the bum said, scratching his nose.

"You're right," Gorodish said, looking at the bum with a glimmering of interest.

"This pigeon you was lookin' at, see, I know him. That's 'cause I got time to live, to look at things, to think. . . ."

"Do you spend most of your time here, in this neighborhood?" Gorodish asked.

"Naw, I keep movin' around. I don't want to develop any what you call 'em, emotional ties. For instance, last week I was in Montrouge. But I got to admit, the Champs-Elysées is more fun. You see some terrific stuff on this street. Where do you live?"

"On the Left Bank."

"That's okay, too, but there's too much competition there. You like Charles Aznavour?"

"Not especially."

"See, now, that's rare: people who don't like Aznavour. I asked you 'cause, see, I don't like Aznavour either. We're gonna get along, Mac. We unnerstan' each other. You got five francs?"

Gorodish pulled out one hundred francs and handed them to the bum.

"You can tell you're not from aroun' here. People aroun' here wouldn' give you the time of day. Thanks. Now I can buy me a case of wine."

"You move around much during the day?"

"You gotta be dumb to move aroun' when everyone else

47

does the movin' for you. I just choose my spot an' siddown an' let it all come to me."

"Where were you yesterday?"

"Right here. I didn' move until nighttime. Then I went to get a bite to eat in the park down the bottom of the avenue."

"Tell me what you saw between, say, six in the evening and the time you left."

"Lotsa things."

"Give me an example."

"Well, I saw a young guy an' his girlfriend, they were fightin', he punched her and the chick went crazy, started beatin' on him so bad two guys hada stop her. That was funny. Then there was a whole busload of Japanese photographed me. I was sittin' here, mindin' my own business, when suddenly they're all aroun' me, clickin' away, click, click, you'd think they'd give me a tip or somethin', but nothing doin'. So I yelled at 'em some an' they left. What else did I see? Oh, yeah, a guy sellin' hot watches. Some cops came an' picked up a girl who lifted a dress in one of the stores, there, behind us. An' Yves Montand walked by, he stopped atta newspaper stand an' bought a magazine, an' a little girl tried to steal a car. . . ."

Startled, Gorodish said, "What did she look like?"

"All white, like fresh outta a car wash."

"The *girl*. What did she look like?"

"You a cop?"

"Hey, do I look like a cop?" Gorodish asked, exasperated.

"Naw, but these days it's hard to tell. The other day there's this girl picked me up, turned out she had a badge an' everythin'. . . ."

"What about the little girl?"

"Real young, all stripedy colors."

"Blond?"

48

"I don't remember hair so good. All I know's she was dressed like a beach umbrella."

"Was she carrying anything?"

"A black plastic bag."

Gorodish knew: it was Alba. He searched in his pockets and pulled out another bill.

"Hey, another hunner' francs . . ." the bum said, grabbing it from Gorodish's hand.

"This is very important," Gorodish said. "I want you to tell me everything you can remember about the little girl."

"The car, it was a white Rolls-Royce, with a gold angel on the radiator cap, you know what I mean? Real high society. I saw 'em get outta the car, an ol' guy with gray hair, real thin, short, big glasses. The other one was a tough-lookin' little sonuvabitch, dressed real well, you know: *chic.* They double-parked the car, left the motor runnin'; I think they went shoppin' inna arcade." The bum pointed toward the Lido Arcade.

"What about the girl?"

"She shows up a minute later, looks atta car, then kinda looks aroun'. Then, jeez, the kid's got some balls, she goes aroun' to the driver's side and gets in. I thought she was gonna take off right away. I kinda wanted to see their faces when they come out an' find the car gone . . . but it looked like to me she didn' know how to drive. After a while, the blond one, you know, the young one? He shows up. I was really afraid for the little girl, but the guy didn' look angry or anythin'. They talk for a while, then the young one gets in behin' the wheel an' the car takes off."

"And the other one? The older man?"

"I didn' see him again. Maybe he walked."

"You didn't happen to notice the license plate?"

"Hey, what is it, you wan' me to give you a photograph an' the car registration number, or what?"

49

"You don't remember anything else?"

"No. Hey, listen, I already gave you a lot, right?"

"That's true."

Gorodish rose, placed his hand on the bum's shoulder and said, "I'm sure we'll meet again."

"All right with me. I'll tell you summa my other stories."

Gorodish hurried to the arcade and went through the men's boutiques one by one, pretending to be a police commissaire investigating a homosexual couple who had been passing bad checks. At last he found the place where the two men had shopped. He had been hoping that they had paid by check; unfortunately, they had paid cash.

Gorodish learned only that the young blond man was very tan, very well built and handsome, except for an ugly scar on his face. The older man had not made much of an impression on the salesgirls, other than the fact that he had paid the bill.

After crying her fill, Alba stepped out of the tub. She knew that she was caught in a trap so perfectly organized that it would be almost impossible to escape. She was afraid, but the worst thing was the idea of Gorodish waiting for her, unable to help. She was still too confused to begin making coherent plans. What worried her most was that she was being given room in which to move around: it was a sure sign of a well-organized security system.

She needed to change her clothes. The colors she had been wearing no longer reflected her mood. Automatically, she opened the armoire. It was empty.

Alba left the bedroom and went up a short stone staircase that led to a large attic. An immense skylight filled one part of the ceiling and the room was bathed in light. There was a large fireplace, shelves full of books, a stereo, records, deep leather club chairs, a bed at the far end of the room, beauti-

50

ful Oriental carpets, a large painting depicting a historic event that she could not identify, small etchings of landscapes, a couch, and a construction that was obviously a turn-of-the-century camera obscura. Alba began to wonder if she was still in France.

Ludovic had a heavy accent; perhaps that was a clue. Alba had just understood something important: the more things she asked for, clothes, records, books, the more chance she would have to discover where she was.

She went back down the small staircase. Four doors opened onto the corridor which was illuminated by a window at its far end. Alba opened a door: a bedroom. She opened another door: the same thing.

When she opened the third door she found herself face-to-face with Charley. He greeted her with his hateful smile. Alba took a step backward.

"Well, sweetie, up and around so soon?"

"Excuse me," Alba said, turning away, but Charley grabbed her sleeve and pulled her toward him.

Alba tried to free herself but Charley twisted her arm and pulled her into the room. He pushed her into the bathroom and snapped open a straight razor directly in front of her eyes.

"See this, sweetie? That's what they used on me. See my face? Look at my face, bitch! You remember: the first little mistake and I'll just *love* cutting you."

Alba began to cry. Brutally, Charley pushed her out into the corridor and slammed his door shut.

Wondering why he hated her so much, Alba dried her tears and went down to the ground floor. She found herself in the entry hall. To the left was a dining room, its windows looking out on the forest and the courtyard. Beyond it was the kitchen. To the right of the entry hall was the large living room.

Alba went into the kitchen. Ludovic was washing aspara-

51

gus. He looked at her, his eyes neutral. At least he did not seem to hate her.

"Lunch in half hour," Ludovic said.

"Where are you from?" Alba asked.

"Zagreb. I don't think Charley wants you hanging around kitchen," Ludovic said, smiling amiably.

Alba went out onto the porch. Charley was there, waiting for her. "Follow me, and listen carefully to what I say. I'm going to show you where you're allowed to go on the grounds."

Keeping her distance, Alba followed Charley around the château, seeing nothing but trees, forest paths and a small green fence about a foot and a half high that marked the outer limit of her territory. All in all there was enough room to move around in, enough room to give her a feeling of a semblance of freedom.

They returned to the château just in time for lunch.

As Alcan drove through Paris he realized that he did not have the soul of a hardened criminal. There were cops in the streets: the sight made him feel as if he were sitting on an anthill. What if someone had seen Alba getting into his terribly white Rolls? Alcan suddenly remembered the name of a garage that specialized in repainting cars in just a few hours. Ten minutes later he had chosen a pale blue color, a perfect match with the blue leather upholstery. Alcan downed several glasses of cognac. He was beginning to feel a little better.

CHAPTER

4

THE OWNER OF THE ROLLS-
Royce dealership obviously thought that the local car
thieves preferred to concentrate their efforts on lesser auto-
mobiles: BMWs or Porsches: It took Gorodish less than a
minute to jimmy the lock and let himself into the display
room. The glorious Rollses shone as if they had just come
from the paint shop and a subtle odor of new leather
caressed his nostrils. Gorodish thought it a shame that the
gleaming monsters could not be dismantled and the parts
sold to some deserving perfectionists who could not afford
an entire automobile.

It was three in the morning. The street was quiet. Gorodish emptied a bottle of honey into the alarm system, then
headed for the office. He pulled out the client files and
began his search. It took him less than ten minutes to find
all the owners of white Rolls-Royces living in and around
Paris: there were only seven. One of them had to be Alba's
kidnapper.

Propping his feet on the manager's desk, Gorodish read through the list of six lucky men and a dead one. His brain hummed like a computer: there was no time to waste researching each of the owners; he had to shake the information loose as quickly as possible. Suddenly, something on the desk caught his eye. It was a telex from a Persian Gulf emirate. The sheik in chief wanted to buy five white Rolls-Royces. The agency's reply was stapled to the order: there would be an eighteen-month wait for delivery.

Gorodish picked up the telephone and dialed the sheik's number. He had to go through fourteen courtiers and retainers but he finally managed to reach the emir, himself.

"You don't know me," Gorodish said. "I am merely a simple, every-day collector of white Rolls-Royces. A friend who works for Rolls told me that you would like to buy five of them."

"Yes," the emir answered in perfect French.

"Fine," Gorodish said. "How would you like to buy seven for the price of five, including several classic models, in perfect condition?"

"Wonderful," the emir said. "Driving a *new* Rolls is so vulgar. How much are you asking?"

"A million and a half francs."

"Do you deliver?"

"No. You may take delivery of the cars tomorrow afternoon. I shall call back, collect, of course, and tell you where."

"You will want the money in cash."

"Naturally."

"Done. And thank you for thinking of me. This evening I will send seven of my chauffeurs to Paris by private jet. They will be accompanied by my secretary, who will bring you the money. Come to think of it, one of my smaller yachts is anchored at Cannes. I believe its hold will easily accommodate my pretty new trinkets."

54

"I'll telephone with the address where you may have the cars picked up."

Gorodish preferred business deals that offered a quick turnaround and no petty bargaining. He flicked on the photocopy machine and left the Rolls agency carrying duplicate files of his seven soon-to-be suppliers.

Charley and Delaborde tore open the heavy cartons and spread their contents—material, plastic bags filled with sequins, gold and silver thread, silks, transparent lightweight plastic sheeting—on the long table in the attic room. Other cartons yielded a sewing machine, scissors, glue, paints and brushes. Delaborde was terribly excited. He had cut a picture of a dragonfly from an entomological journal and shown it to Charley. The younger man had once worked in a fashion house and was happy to be dabbling in his favorite pastime again: tailoring, working with materials, matching colors, sewing.

"Do you really think you can make this?"

"I don't see why not," Charley said. "We have everything we need. The wings will be the hardest part, but as far as the body is concerned, I could make a very tight sheath of black velvet, cover it with sequins, and the strapless top can be made of lamé. I'll use silver silk chiffon for the wings and we can paint on the veins, or I can do them in sequins. I'll make a turban the same color as the sheath and we can glue on plastic domes for the eyes and cover them with black sequins. What do you think?"

"Marvelous! Absolutely marvelous! I have some Japanese tapes of insect sounds, buzzing, humming, chirping, fluttering wings, oh, it's a wonderful cassette! The only thing we need now is a full moon."

They set to work. Luckily, Charley remembered everything he had learned during his two-year apprenticeship in a high fashion house. He had been taught to work without a

55

pattern and now cut directly into the velvet. Delaborde was almost hysterical with anticipation.

The next morning, at the start of business hours, Gorodish rented a warehouse in an isolated area outside Paris, thus ensuring that the comings and goings of those splendid white ladies would not attract undue attention.

That afternoon he inspected the ladies' living quarters: only three of them slept in cozy garages; the others were forced to content themselves with the vulgar promiscuity of the street.

Gorodish had hot-wired more than one car in his life, but stealing seven Rolls-Royces in one night demanded the assistance of other practitioners of the art.

Keeping the easier targets for himself, two superb models built in the 1960s, Gorodish wended his way to the Clichy area in central Paris. It was the cocktail hour. In a nondescript café he made the acquaintance of two young apprentices in the trade who, in turn, recruited three of their more talented colleagues. Five thousand francs per man was offered and accepted, after which Gorodish invited them all to join him for a simple yet elegant Japanese dinner.

Later, Gorodish dropped them off at their assigned theaters of operations. They had merely to steal a Rolls and deliver it to the warehouse, where they would receive the second half of the fee. Gorodish counted himself lucky to have found a market for the masterpieces even before having liberated them.

A little after nine o'clock, Gorodish's major coconspirator left his modest twelve-room apartment on the Place des Vosges. An A and R man at a record company, he was wearing a pair of old jeans, a silk shirt, several days' growth of beard, dark glasses and long white hair. The A and R man stopped en route to pick up a delicious young creature

56

young enough to be his granddaughter (undoubtedly an aspiring singer) and happily accompanied her to a fashionable restaurant. The Rolls he had stolen remained double-parked outside, the parking attendant having been instructed to do anything that might add to the prestige of the establishment.

A large tip helped place Gorodish at the next table. As he munched on an *oeuf en gelée*, he eavesdropped on the happy couple, listening as each of them desperately did his (or her) number on the other. The night was filled with veiled promises. The problem was that the lovely creature, whose name was Lea, really did expect a recording contract.

By meal's end, four hands had managed to fray a path through the forest of bottles, mustard pots and other impediments to love. Bitterly, Gorodish reflected that in the United States a car was stolen once every twenty-eight seconds. What could one do when one lived in an ancient civilization in which the simplest act implied subtexts of meaning and convolutions of intent? What could one do without drive-ins, fast-food joints and instant sex? Gorodish sensed that one day he would have to cross the Atlantic. He made a solemn vow that he would take his adorable angel with him: that is, if he ever managed to find her.

The gleaming white lady stood alone on the dark street. The play of shadows restored the dignity that had been stripped from her by the ignoble deals to which she had been witness. Gorodish opened the door, lifted the hood and gently stripped a few wires. The delicate sound of the pistons echoed in the night. Gorodish emptied the ashtray: he hated the odor of dead cigars.

Alba's curiosity was aroused. Charley and Louis had locked themselves in the attic room. Ludovic had left to go shopping, taking Alba's list with him after Delaborde had approved the items on it. She had ordered jeans, three T-shirts, sandals, underpants, two shirts, a sweat suit, jogging shoes, socks, a sweater and the short stories of de Maupassant in paperback.

Alba had decided not only to continue jogging, but to find a way of intensifying her training sessions without being seen. She was determined to be in such physical shape that any escape attempt she finally made would have a better chance of succeeding. Alba had a vague plan in mind, but she needed more information: there were too many pieces missing.

The plan was very simple. One day she would cross the limits of the territory to which she had been confined and run as far as the edge of the property. Before trying it, however, she had to know how far the property extended and what sort of obstacle she would face at the boundary. Maybe there was a wall or a fence. The one thing she feared, besides Charley, was the dogs. Despite the fact that they terrified her, Alba forced herself to spend part of each day at the kennel, talking to the animals, getting them used to her, even secretly feeding them.

Alba had hoped to discover where she was being held through a forgotten wrapping from a local dairy, a label in an article of clothing or from a local store address printed on a grocery bag. Up to now all the food had been removed from its containers before being served. The kitchen was off limits to her; and in any case the meat locker and pantry were kept locked.

Still, Alba kept watch, knowing that one day or another a sign, an indication, would escape her captors' attention. The château had no radio, no television. There were no newspapers, and the telephone never rang. Alba felt completely cut off from the world.

*　*　*

Flora was almost seventy years old and looked every bit her age. She came staggering out of her favorite bar at closing time, navigating down the street like a rum-laden galleon that had drunk its own cargo. Happily, the street was a good twenty-five feet wide and empty of traffic. Flora was wearing a black dress that seemed to be having a hard time keeping up with her as she stumbled along, holding a pair of high-heeled crocodile pumps in her hand.

Gorodish followed her, knowing that he dared not let her drive the Rolls. He could not turn over a deflowered car body to the emir: those desert tribesmen were extremely punctilious in matters of morality.

Suddenly, inspiration struck. "Flora, Flora," Gorodish called.

Flora stopped and turned, smiling unsteadily. Gorodish took her in his arms. "How wonderful to see you again after all these years," he said.

Flora stared up at him, a bemused smile on her lips. "Sorry . . . drunk as a skunk . . . don't recognize . . ."

"It's extraordinary, Flora! We've found each other at last!"

"Who? What's your name, honey? Maybe I did . . ."

"Arthur."

"Oh, yeah, Arthur . . . I think maybe I . . ."

"Do you still live on Avenue Victor Hugo."

"Sure . . . my car's over there. Could you drive me home?"

After one last drink, Gorodish tucked Flora into bed, kissed her on the forehead and then drove back to the warehouse where the six other Rolls-Royces awaited him.

One of them was blue. Its paint was not quite dry.

The château stood silhouetted against the full moon. For more than an hour now Delaborde had been moving feverishly around the grounds, growing ever more excited the

59

longer he walked. The costume was fantastic. The enormous dragonfly was undoubtedly waiting for him. He had given orders that she be made ready, that she wait for him. Everything was to begin at midnight: the insect noises, the dragonfly, soaring, moonlit, beneath the skylight, the fire in the fireplace, the black satin sheets. Delaborde paced back and forth, inhaling the resinous odor of the forest, visualizing the superb anthills that undoubtedly stood among the trees in the deepest part of the woods. It was almost time. He turned back toward the château. The moon shone brightly in his eyes, illuminating his pale, deadly face.

Delaborde ran up the stairs, moving in rhythm to the insect hum coming from the attic room.

They had forced Alba into the sheath, dressed her in the strapless top, the long gloves, the wings, the turban with its sequined, faceted, monstrous eyes. The strange costume chilled her. Helpless, trembling, she hung from a track that had been installed in the ceiling as horrible, rasping noises came pouring from the loudspeakers. The sight of the black, satin-covered bed, the emptiness of the room, the milky light glistening on the sequins, on the wings, on her shoulders, on the slopes of her breasts and her bare arms, terrified her. She turned her eyes away from the mirrors lining the room and uttered a hoarse, muffled cry: "Serge!"

A few seconds later Delaborde entered the room. He locked the door and walked slowly toward Alba hanging beneath the skylight. She shuddered.

"Luna, my marvelous insect, you're trembling. You must not be afraid. We are going to be so happy together."

Delaborde walked over to the amplifier and turned the sound up even higher.

"You're nuts!" Alba said.

Slowly, he advanced toward her, revealing his teeth in a terrifying smile. His hands reached up toward her.

60

Alba tried desperately to free herself, but the leather band around her waist held her firmly to the track. Below her, Delaborde was sliding deeper into his macabre fantasies.

"The track goes round and round, oh, it's wonderful, my Luna . . . we shall indulge ourselves in the ecstatic foreplay that precedes the moment of copulation. But before we join together in the ecstasy of the mating flight, I must instruct you further. . . ."

Delaborde walked over to the bookcase and took out an antique volume bound in leather. Placing himself directly beneath Alba, he opened the book and said in a quavering voice:

"I hold in my hand a treasury of eighteenth-century intelligence, scientific observation and intellectual subtlety, written by René de Réaumur, one of the great minds of the French Enlightenment. I want you to listen carefully as I read the passage that concerns us. I want you to understand that I am completely, utterly, subject to your will. . . ."

"The Female which flutters coyly in the Air will shortly have a Train of Males in attendance upon her, and if she should alight upon some Leaf or Stalk, will not be long alone. A Male will straightway seek her out, flying above and about her (for the Male ever keeps directly above the Female, whether at rest or on the Wing). Then at first he does hover above her Head, since it is his Intent to approach so closely as to enable him to take hold of her with his Legs. Directly he has her in his Grasp, then he curls up his body so as to bring his hinder Parts to touch the Neck of the Female, and even at that Moment does grapple her to him in such a wise that she no longer has the power to take leave of him. The body of the Male terminates in a pair of Great Hooks, or Claspers, the which are blunt at the tips. These he spreads wide so as to grip the Female by the Neck, as it

might be with a pair of Pincers, and draws them together as straitly as is necessary to ascertain that she is incapable of making an Escape.

"But 'though the Male has gripp'd the Female in this masterful Embrace it is beyond his power alone to consummate the Nuptials. We have observed that the requisite Parts of the Male are situated on the underside of the Abdomen, quite near the armoured plates of the Corselet, but yet some Distance from the hinder Parts of the Female. For their Coupling to be accomplished, the Female must wish it so, and it is left her to do what must be done. Even so, it appears to have been ordained by Natural Law that the Female shall only give herself to the Male after having offered some Resistance. Among the Insects, excepting only the Queen Bee, all appear to reject the Male's initial Caresses; the Damselfly also seems at first to be ill disposed to yield to the advances of her Consort. . . .

"When the Female can resist no longer the prolonged Entreaties of the Male, when she at last is determined to have done that for which she has shown so little Relish and for some time heretofore, she inclines her body backward . . . and extends it beneath the Abdomen of the Male, who, for his part, tarries not in arching his body like a Bow. But scarcely has she drawn her hinder Parts toward the center of the Abdomen of the Male but that, as if she had thought better on't, she draws them back again and resumes her initial Stance. It is no more than an instant before she bends her body back once more, still farther than before, and after two or three such attempts, she at last places her hinder Parts on that very Spot on the Abdomen of the Male where those organs are to be found that are fitted to receive them. If she has not alit upon the very Spot, she draws herself a little farther back or forward, as may be wanted."

* * *

62

"Shove it up your ass," Alba shouted.

"Oh, Luna, your passionate frenzy touches my soul! It is so scrupulously, entomologically correct. I know now that I was right to choose you: your intuition will help you re-create the female's exact emotions when the male's pheromones lure her into the mating flight. . . ."

Delaborde stripped off his clothes and pulled on a costume that resembled the one Alba was wearing. Then he climbed up a small stepladder and hooked himself into a contraption similar to the one from which she was hanging. The only difference seemed to be that Delaborde's apparatus had a motor.

A black satin strap linked his ankles. Delaborde parted his knees and looped the strap around Alba's neck. She cried out, frightened by the strap, by the amplified insect sounds, the rasping noises pounding ever more loudly against her ears.

Delaborde turned on the motor and they began to slide around the room, the pattern of their flight determined by the meanderings of the ceiling track. Delaborde felt as if his soul was bathing in sound. He uttered small, strident cries, trying to harmonize with the symphony of grinding, scraping noises surrounding them.

Alba dragged along beside him, twisting and contorting as she tried to free herself of the soft noose around her neck. She stared at Delaborde's ridiculous costume, desperately hoping that his imagination would be so inflamed by the setting and the flight that he would not actually attempt to mate with her.

At that moment she swore to herself that someday she would kill him.

Delaborde watched Alba's reflection in the mirrors lining the flight path. The moon shone down on them, illuminating the hidden crevices of her body.

63

"Luna, you are a prisoner of my desire . . . your body gleams . . . your eyes are driving me mad . . . and, oh, those traces of blue and green glinting on your wings . . . it's so beautiful. . . ."

After what seemed an eternity of aeronautic frenzy, the motor gave off a few puffs of smoke and an odor of burning plastic began to fill the room. To Alba's relief, the mating flight ground to a halt.

Delaborde shrieked. He climbed down the ladder and stood beneath Alba, staring up at her as she hung there, glowing in the milky light of the moon. Suddenly, he was shaken by a solitary delirium.

Afterward, laughing madly, he helped her down. Alba recoiled from his touch.

"Come, Luna, let me take you in my arms."

Slowly, he advanced on her. "I see you trying to flee, my Luna, and the moon shines on your fragile body. Your eyes, your eyes. Your quivering wings. I'll be gentle with you, Luna. I won't drive a pin through your pale body. I love you too much for that, my Luna. I love the brush of your wings, the fragility of your body, the quivering of your antennae."

Delaborde circled around her. Alba felt like an insect caught in a spider's web.

Suddenly, Delaborde threw himself on her, holding her tightly as Alba tried to fight him off, scratching his face, hitting him. Delaborde would not let go: he dragged her to the bed and threw her on it.

Alba began to shriek, kicking out at him, her slim white legs tearing free of the sheath.

"That's it, my beauty, give me your sweet body."

He did not seem to feel the blood running down his face, nor the pain of Alba's fingernails ripping his skin. He clung to her like a punch-drunk boxer, too groggy to feel the punishing blows raining down on him.

Suddenly he let go of Alba and began shredding the silver

and gold strapless top, ripping it away until Alba's breasts were naked. She lay on a pile of broken wings, sequins clinging to her sweaty skin as Delaborde's disgusting hands ran over her. Her screams echoed in the room, the stone walls seeming to absorb the sound.

"That's it, my Luna, scream louder, scream louder, my Luna, my love, my Lunaloveluna."

Delaborde tore at his shirt, sliding his naked torso against her sweat-slick body. Alba wriggled from his grasp as Delaborde's blood flowed down onto her breasts. All at once he bit her so fiercely that she shrieked. Delaborde felt as if his eardrums were exploding.

Suddenly he realized that if he did not protect himself she was quite capable of killing him. He was bleeding in several places now, the pain making the blood seethe in his veins. Delaborde punched the dragonfly, hitting her until at last her nails stopped raking his face. Then he peeled off what was left of his clothing.

Alba took advantage of the brief respite to try to roll off the bed, away from the revolting, blood-soaked sheets. Delaborde fell on her, shouting unintelligibly as he pressed against her with the full weight of his body.

Alba felt as if she were suffocating, the screams catching in her throat as the torn material on which she lay knotted around her like netting. The pudgy body on top of her went into convulsions. Delaborde was shrieking, the words meaningless, except for the chant of "Luna, Luna," and the sound of something that sounded like a death rattle vibrating in his throat.

Delaborde went limp and collapsed on top of her. Gathering the last of her strength, Alba punched him full in the face with every ounce of energy left in her. Then she fainted.

65

CHAPTER

5

GORODISH THREW HIMSELF ON his bed, too weak even to undress. Physical exhaustion, emotional pain and anger were draining him.

After only a few hours' sleep, a terrible nightmare brought Gorodish awake. In his dream he had seen Alba dying in a ditch, her body covered with maggots, dried leaves and crawling insects. As he sat up on the edge of the bed he imagined he could still hear her cries, and even more frightening images filled his imagination.

It took him a good fifteen minutes to pull himself together and another ten minutes to put some order in his thoughts. He listened to the answering machine: nobody had called.

Gorodish brewed a cup of coffee. As he drank it, he decided to shave. The sight of his worn face in the mirror was a shock: he looked as if he had aged ten years. After a hot shower, he went back into the living room, feeling the apartment empty of all life, empty of energy since Alba's disappearance. The piano looked like a coffin. He opened the thermos bottle and poured himself yet another cup of coffee. When he went into the kitchen for the cream, he saw the yellow banana Nesquik can standing on the counter. The bitter sting of tears filled his eyes, overflowed and spilled down his face into his mouth.

The green plants in the kitchen needed watering but Gorodish did not have the strength to deal with them. As far back as he could remember, he had never known such pain. A headache was flashing behind his eyes. He took three aspirin, changed his clothes and left the apartment.

Gorodish turned over the seven Rolls-Royces to the emir's representative, apologizing that one was blue. In exchange, he was handed a small valise filled with money. Too distracted to count it, he decided this one time to trust in the sincerity of strangers.

Later that afternoon, Gorodish went to a lecture at the Sorbonne. The amphitheater was filled with students waiting to be mesmerized as Alcan, high priest of postmodern psychoanalytic theory and owner of a newly painted Rolls-Royce delivered one of his rare lectures to those select few who could almost understand him.

"I need not point out," Alcan began, "that my decision to bare myself before you today will be interpreted in certain circles as an act of perversity on my part, a symbolic punctuation in the stream of constancy of evolving thought: real, therefore impossible. But then, what eccentricities have not been imputed to me in these troubled times? Your presence here reassures me that you have not mis-understood the significance of my gesture.

"Shall we begin?

"The inextricability of various aspects of the functions I have previously discussed has led me to formulate a conclusion which I deliver up to you in the following, dare I say, lapidary phrase: 'Pleasure is the sagacity of the spurt.' "

The students expressed joy at the news. The Master of

67

Psychoanalytic Theory nodded his head slightly in response to their applause, and withdrew.

Gorodish followed Alcan, watching his every movement and gesture. After only a few seconds he came to the conclusion that the man knew where Alba had been taken. But he could not force Alcan to reveal her whereabouts: he would have to invent a more subtle method of obtaining the information. Gorodish decided to trap the psychoanalyst in the labyrinth of his own theories.

Gorodish returned to his own apartment and telephoned Alcan's office. He insisted that the secretary give him an appointment for the next day. Impossible: booked solid. Gorodish persisted, demanding to speak to Alcan, who, when he picked up the receiver, reminded Gorodish that Freud, *himself,* never set a specific time for appointments but usually received patients between three and four in the afternoon.

Delaborde staggered as he rose from the bed. He looked down at Alba's unconscious body, and scattered images from the preceding night filled his mind. He ached all over and his face was swollen. Delaborde went into the bathroom and held a cold compress against his bruised face. Then he combed his hair, brushed his teeth, put on a silk bathrobe and went down to breakfast.

Charley was running a vacuum cleaner in the living room. After all, Delaborde thought, he was being paid to take care of the house, too.

Charley had enjoyed listening to Alba scream during the night. When Delaborde came downstairs, he turned off the vacuum cleaner, hoping to hear details of what had happened.

Delaborde sat down at the dining-room table. Charley followed him into the room, took one look at his face and said, "Oh, the bitch. She really did a job on you."

68

"I don't mind. It was wonderful."

"She's a cunt."

"She'd have killed me if I'd let her," Delaborde said happily.

"You ought to turn her over to me for a while. I'd tame her for you. You can't let her get away with this."

Delaborde smiled painfully.

"Where is she?" Charley demanded.

"Asleep, in my bed."

"You can't go through this every night; you'll wind up looking like Frankenstein's monster."

"You're right, Charley, but I don't want her damaged."

Ludovic came out of the kitchen carrying a large silver tray holding tea, toast, honey, butter and a glass of orange juice. When he saw Delaborde's face he hesitated for a moment, but did not say a word.

"I'm so hungry I could eat a horse," Delaborde said. "Bring me some roast beef, Ludovic." Delaborde gulped down a piece of toast. "I don't mind fighting with Luna, you know; but I think I'd have even more pleasure, a different kind of pleasure, if she was more cooperative. I'm worried what the painter will say. He's never going to be able to do the portrait if she refuses to pose, or if she carries on like she did last night."

"What painter?" Charley frowned.

"Oh, that's right, I haven't told you about him yet. There's nothing to worry about, he's part of the organization. It's the man who forged the identity papers."

"You mean Marco? I didn't know he was a painter."

"Oh, he's a very good artist. I'm going to bring him here to paint a portrait of Luna. We'll dress her up in the costume . . ."

"It's dangerous to bring in someone from the outside. That'll make another person who knows you're here. I think you ought to forget about it."

69

"We can arrange things so he doesn't know where he is, can't we?"

"It won't be easy. But maybe we can work something out. I'll have to keep an eye on him every minute he's here." Charley pondered the problem. "When do you want him to come?"

"As soon as he can."

"Okay. You call and tell him to be at the Limoges train station at whatever time you decide on, and I'll pick him up. We'll blindfold him before bringing him here."

"That's a good idea. Let me have the telephone."

The painter answered the telephone at the second ring. His voice sounded tired and dull.

"Good morning. This is Louis Garrard."

"Hello. You still want me to do the painting?"

"That's why I'm calling. Everything's ready now. You must come here immediately."

"I can't. I've begun work on a canvas for an exhibition."

"That's too bad. There's a full moon now. If you don't come we'll have to wait another whole month. . . ."

"How large a painting did you want?"

"Something big. Say, three feet by seven feet, something like that."

"It'd take at least ten days to do a painting that size."

"I don't mind."

"It'll cost you."

"How much?"

"At least twenty thousand francs."

"I'll give you thirty thousand if you come today."

"I'm on my way. I think I have a prepared canvas that'll do, somewhere here in the studio."

"What time will you leave Paris?"

"Around eleven."

"Take the train to Limoges and . . ."

"I can't travel on the train with a canvas that big and all my painting supplies. I'll have to take my station wagon."

"Well, if you must . . . Let's see, I'll send Charley and Ludovic to meet you at the train station in Limoges around six this evening."

"All right. See you then."

Delaborde placed two slices of roast beef on a piece of toast and began to chew. "I want both of you to go meet him."

"Okay," Charley said. "Do you want me to take care of the girl now?"

"Yes. We can't allow her to ruin the posing sessions with her hysterics. Is there enough time to tame the little tigress between now and when Marco gets here?"

"No problem."

"Really?"

"You have my guarantee."

"How extraordinary. But I don't want any marks on her face or arms or chest. I don't want Marco to think we've been torturing her."

Charley smiled. He drank a cup of tea and then went upstairs to waken the nymph.

Someone was pulling her hair. Alba cried out and her heart began to pound. Without thinking, she kicked out at the form bending over her but her feet never reached their target. At that moment she recognized Charley and went cold. She tried to slide to the far side of the bed but he held on, gripping her arm.

"No more of that," he snapped. "Get up."

Charley pulled her from the bed, his fury growing as he saw the ruined moth costume. "Go to your room!"

Alba walked in front of him, trembling as she felt his hateful gaze following every movement of her body.

71

He closed the bedroom door. "You're disgusting," Charley said. "Take off your clothes and wash yourself."

Alba took a step toward the bathroom but Charley stopped her, ordering her to strip in front of him. She hesitated for a moment, then sensing that Charley was about to explode, obeyed him. The sheath was difficult to peel off, the wings awkward to remove, but at last she stood naked under his icy gaze.

Alba showered, washing off the sequins still clinging to her skin, and the dried, sticky mess on her chest. She came back into the bedroom wrapped in a towel.

Charley was seated in the armchair. "Come here," he said.

Alba began to shake. He stared at her for a long time. "Raise your arms over your head," he said finally.

Alba did as she was told. Charley pulled the bath towel away and settled back into the chair, lighting a cigarette and smoking it down to a butt without saying a word. Alba was paralyzed with dread, trembling at the thought that he might burn her. But he did nothing. Finally, he crushed out the cigarette butt, tossing back his curly blond hair.

Then he punched her in the pit of the stomach. Alba fell to the floor. Charley sat down again and waited until she stopped gasping. When she was able to breathe again he said coldly, "Get up."

Alba got to her feet and edged away from him.

"Get back here," Charley rasped.

Alba obeyed him. There was a great emptiness within her, as if she was about to die.

"I'll use the razor next time. You listen: you belong to me now. There will be no more scenes like the one last night, unless he wants you to resist, understand? You'll do exactly as you're told, or I will personally see to you. I don't care how long it takes, but when I'm through with you, you'll be broken. You understand? Nothing'll show on the outside; but you'll be broken."

Alba did not say a word.

"Answer me: do you understand?"

"Yes," she said slowly.

"Okay. Now, there's a man coming to paint you. You'll do whatever he says, pose however he wants. At the first sign of rebellion, you and I will have ourselves a private session, just the two of us. I'll be here when you pose, so you be careful what you say. Now, I want you to get dressed, go downstairs and apologize for your behavior. You promise that it'll never happen again and tell him that you'll do whatever he wants you to from now on. Ludovic will give you some pills. I want you to sleep until tonight. I'm going to try to fix the costume. You take better care of it next time: I've worked hard making it and it means a lot to me."

Charley left the room. Giving in to her terror, Alba collapsed on the bed, tears streaming down her face.

Gorodish thought the interior of Alcan's office looked like the inside of a cigar box. The analyst moved out from behind his mahogany desk. There was a sad and weary expression on his face as he shook Gorodish's hand.

"Take off your jacket," Alcan said, "you'll be more comfortable."

"I'm not wearing a jacket."

Alcan's tired eyes focused on Gorodish and he realized that the new patient was wearing a pair of jeans and a T-shirt with Freud's face emblazoned across it.

"Where did you get that?" Alcan asked.

"*He* gave it to me," Gorodish said. "We're good friends."

"You mean that *he, himself,* gives out T-shirts with *his* picture on them?"

"Yes."

73

Alcan scratched his nose. "It seems somewhat vulgar, but *he's* the boss, after all. I think I'll order a couple thousand of them with my own picture. . . ."

"Good idea," Gorodish said; "they'll look nice on some of your young female students: your eyes centered over their breasts."

"Disciples," Alcan said, finicky about the correct use of language.

"Forgive me."

"Never ask for forgiveness. Now, where were we, oh, yes: my eyes riveted on those mounds of . . . no, toward an ever more profound understanding of . . ."

"Would you like me to talk to the printer about the T-shirts?" Gorodish offered.

"How very kind of you. My secretary will give you a free eight-by-ten glossy. . . . Now, won't you lay down on the couch?"

"I prefer the armchair."

"As you wish. . . . I recognize your need to return to the fetal position. . . ."

Gorodish turned the armchair so that it was facing Alcan. He wanted to watch the man.

"I am a strict Freudian," Alcan continued, "which means that although you may have my complete attention, I shall not speak."

They fell silent. Gorodish stared at Alcan. Alcan stared back. After a few minutes he looked down at the blank sheet of paper on his desk. Three more minutes passed. Alcan delicately picked up his pen and wrote:

"Oh, shit, another one of those. Name-of-the-Father, Father Freud, how long must I endure the paranoid fantasies of subject-objects such as these, whose only aim in life is to make me believe that I shall never be that which I think I am to become?"

Then Alcan drew a Christmas tree. Then he decorated its branches with balls and candy canes. Then he stared at his handiwork for a while. Twenty minutes flew by. Although he had often professed disdain for Buddha, Alcan managed to fall into an absolutely Nirvanalike trance.

Suddenly he rose and disappeared into the next office. His secretary entered the room, presented Gorodish with the bill for the day's session and graciously granted him another appointment for two days later.

CHAPTER

6

STRANGE EMOTIONS FILLED
Gorodish as he moved through the city of Vienna, home of
Beethoven, Schubert, Webern and so many other artists.
But it was the genius of Dr. Sigmund Freud that had
brought him here.

He found 19 Berggasse, the home of the Father of Psy-
choanalysis for fifty years until the Nazis came to power. It
was now a museum.

At three in the morning Gorodish returned and made his
way into the flower-filled courtyard. He looked up at the
third-floor windows. A little exercise wouldn't hurt him and
the heavy stone walls would provide excellent handholds.
Gorodish climbed up to the small balcony, smashed a pane
of glass and opened the window.

He moved slowly through the apartment, unable to resist
stretching out for a moment on the famous rug-covered
divan. The room was filled with Greek, Roman, Etruscan,
Oriental and Egyptian statues, among them a small bronze

figure of the Egyptian god, Horus. Horus was always represented as having the head of a falcon, and Gorodish remembered reading that Freud had noted down a dream he had had in childhood, one in which he had seen two or three bird-headed creatures carrying off his mother. Gorodish was certain the statuette would impress Alcan.

He felt strangely reluctant to leave the apartment, but this was no time to be self-indulgent.

On the plane back to Paris, Gorodish leafed through a biography of Freud, hoping to learn something more about the man's life and work that would be of help in his plans.

The posing sessions lasted late into the night. Alba was exhausted but she was safe, at least temporarily, from Delaborde's attentions. For the time being he appeared to have transferred his passions to the image of the dragonfly slowly evolving on the canvas.

In the beginning Charley sat in on every posing session in the attic room, but he soon became bored. Eventually he began to leave Alba and Marco alone. As the nights passed, a friendship sprang up between the artist and his model. Marco had become fascinated with Alba's moonlit beauty and often fell into a state of ecstatic contemplation, his gaze caressing her body as if, in some way, he yearned to protect her. Something magical began to happen to the portrait but, inevitably, Charley's sudden appearances broke the spell. Marco saw Alba's terror each time Charley came near her. The young man's presence affected him strangely, too, turning his fingers awkward and ruining his usual dexterity with the brushes. Finally, Marco demanded that the blond watchdog be forbidden access to the attic room, going so far as to threaten to stop work on the painting unless he was left alone with Alba-Luna.

At last Delaborde gave in, promising not to look at the

77

portrait until it was finished. Now the canvas began to come to life, began to vibrate with energy. Alba marveled at the gradual transformation, her fascination almost making her forget that she was a prisoner. Marco rarely spoke as he worked, but when dawn changed the dragonfly back into a girl, when sunlight replaced the milky glow of the moon, they would talk quietly, almost whispering so as not to be overheard.

At first the painter had tried to avoid becoming attached to Alba: it was far too risky. But little by little she managed to bewitch him, to seduce him, to move him, to awaken his curiosity. As the work progressed, and Marco's soul blended into the colors on the canvas, he began to understand Alba's despair at being the object of Louis's passions. And he could feel Charley's hatred for the girl. The mere idea of the violence that had been done to her was unbearable.

As the allotted ten days drew to an end, Alba was forced to pose for longer and longer periods. Her body ached from the enforced immobility of the pose, but strangely enough she felt a sense of inner peace, in sharp contrast to the anxious nights in which she cried herself to sleep. Her mind seemed to detach itself from her body and she projected her thoughts toward Gorodish, sending him telepathic messages of anguish and passion.

Oftentimes, when posing, she actually managed to ignore the passing hours; at other times she felt as if she were dead. Marco liked classical music and often listened to the Haydn sonatas while he worked. Each time the music began Alba tried to hold back her tears but, with the first notes of the piano, she would break down, Marco taking advantage of her despair to capture every nuance of her pain in the tears streaming down her face. The portrait had become sublime.

One day, as dawn broke and the room, which smelled of paint thinner, veered to a lighter shade of blue, Marco

78

rubbed his eyes, shook the strain from his arms and said, "It's finished." There was a note of sadness in his voice.

"Finished?"

"Yes. Come take a look."

Alba stepped down from the dais where Marco had placed the red velvet couch. She stared at the portrait and then began to weep quietly. Marco took her in his arms.

"Don't leave me here," she said; "they're going to kill me."

"Don't cry, Alba; I'll take you with me. I'll never again be able to paint anything but your body and your face. We'll run away together, Alba. I'll give you a new identity, a new name, a new life. We'll go far away, to America maybe. I have a gallery there. We'll forget everything that's happened here and make a new life for ourselves."

Alba held Marco tightly. She admired the painter, but the embrace was a lie.

"We'll have to watch out for Charley," Alba whispered. "He's dangerous. And he said he'd cut my face if I tried to run away. And there's the alarm system, and the dogs. . . ."

"Is there a wall or a fence around the property?" Marco asked.

"I don't know. All they told me is that the alarm will go off if I walk past a certain point. They've let me move around in an area about a thousand feet around the château, but I don't know how far the gate is. In any case, the gate opens from inside the château, and it has a separate alarm system."

"Do Charley and Ludovic have guns?"

"Probably. But the worst thing is that I don't even know where I am. I don't even know if we're still in France."

"I know where we are, more or less," Marco said. "They picked me up at the train station in Limoges. They blind-

79

folded me, but I know we didn't come too far, two hours' drive at most."

"You don't have a gun, do you?"

"No, but if the gate isn't too heavy we can try to crash through it with my car, or we can climb up on the roof and make it over the wall. By the time they woke up and reached the gate we'd have a good head start. You look as if you could run fast, if you had to."

"I've been training," Alba said.

"If we can just make it to the forest we have a good chance of getting away, but we'll have to make sure we don't lose each other in the dark."

"I'll wear my sweat suit," Alba said. "It's dark blue."

"How do they get the dogs out of the kennel?"

"There's an automatic door that opens when the alarm goes off."

"I'll have to wire it closed; they won't think of checking it. And I'll take the distributor head off the R-16; that ought to give us a little more of an edge."

"When can we leave?" Alba asked. "I'm so scared something's going to happen."

"Tonight. Louis is giving a little party to celebrate my finishing the painting. Let's hope they all get drunk and fall asleep before morning."

"Why don't we leave when Charley goes to do the shopping? He's always gone at least two hours, and there'd only be Ludovic to worry about."

"I think we'd have a better chance in the dark. We'll lose them in the woods and head for a village. . . ."

"I've made up so many escape plans that now I'm scared to try it," Alba said. "I don't know how to explain it, it's just that I'm so . . ."

"I know. We'd better get some sleep now. And it'd be safer if we didn't spend too much time together. You sleep as late as you can and try not to draw attention to yourself at the party. Act the way you usually do: you know, vague and absent. Go to bed when everybody else does, but be ready to leave. I'll come get you when everything's set."

"What about the dogs? They know me, they don't even bark anymore when I come near the kennel. They'll wake everybody up if you try wiring the door shut. I'd better do it."

"Okay," Marco said. "I have everything we'll need in the car. While you're taking care of the dogs I'll disable the R-16. But remember, if anything goes wrong, don't wait: head for the car."

"All right."

Alba hugged Marco again. Then she went to her bedroom, pulled the drapes closed and lay down on the bed. Her mind was seething with images, ideas, plans, but at last she managed to calm down. She uttered one brief prayer for the success of the escape, then fell asleep.

Gorodish bolted awake in the middle of the night. He had dreamed that Alba was back, that she lay asleep in her bedroom. He turned on the bedside lamp, rose, crossed the corridor and opened the door to her room. The overhead light glared down on the empty bed. A copy of *Red Harvest*, by Dashiell Hammett, lay on the nightstand.

Gorodish opened the closet door and took out the clothing Alba had been wearing the last time he held her. Embracing the garments, he buried his face in them, breathing deeply of her scent. Then he slipped into Alba's sleeping bag and, holding her clothing against his heart, began to sob.

Gorodish sat down facing Alcan. Fighting back an urge to grab the man by the throat and choke the truth out of him,

81

Gorodish pulled a T-shirt from a plastic bag and handed it across the desk. The picture on the T-shirt showed Alcan and Freud, side by side.

Moved, Alcan stared at it. "Thank you," he said. "What a nice gesture."

"My pleasure," Gorodish said. He rummaged through his pockets and pulled out the small statuette of Horus he had stolen from Freud's apartment in Vienna. He handed the statuette to Alcan, who took it with trembling hands.

Gorodish allowed him to examine it for a few minutes. "*He* gave it to me, for you."

"What?"

"The last time I was here I had the impression that you did not understand the purpose of my visit. . . ."

"What kind of carnival con-game . . ."

"I've heard it said that *he* appears in your dreams quite often. . . ."

"Uh, well, yes. . . ."

"And that you have always listened to *him*, that *he* has guided you on your path, in your research, and has been the primary inspiration behind more than a few of your discoveries. . . ."

"I have never denied *his* profound influence on my . . ."

"But you must have sensed that it was more than that. There must have been times when you felt the merging of your two personalities. . . ."

Alcan went pale. "I admit that there were times . . ."

"Let's get down to facts," Gorodish continued. "*He* told me to arrange a meeting between the two of you. *He* has recently made an unusual discovery which *he* wishes to communicate to you. Obviously, you are free to refuse: *he* will not pressure you in any way. But I dare say I can speak for *him* when I say that *he* would be happy to turn over to you the results of all the research *he* has undertaken during these long years of silence. Of course this must remain a secret among the three of us."

Alcan stared at the statuette, his face ashen. "Why didn't *he* speak to me directly," he whined.

"*He* knew that you would have doubts. And there are several small heresies that have cropped up in your work lately that have troubled *him* . . . that last seminar, for instance. . . ."

"I was merely stating certain reservations . . ."

"Exactly. *He* took it very badly. While we're on the subject, I believe *he's* quite angry with you: something about your behavior these last few weeks. . . ."

"Really?" Alcan said, sounding like a naughty child.

"I believe that a full and frank explanation is the only way . . ."

"If you really think . . ." Alcan hesitated. "How do I get in touch with *him?*"

"Be at the shopping mall at Parly II, on the outskirts of Paris, tonight. . . ."

"You mean *he'll* be there in the flesh?"

"What did you think I was talking about: a medium, a Ouija board?"

"You can never tell with *him.*"

"*He'll* be there in person."

"We must alert the media."

"You know how *he* hates publicity. *He* wants a private meeting, just the two of you."

"It's such a strange place for a meeting. Perhaps if I invited *him* to dinner . . ."

"*He* specifically asked for an out-of-the-way place. . . ."

"Am I authorized to publish an account of the meeting?"

"I don't know. Be at the bookstore in the shopping mall at eight o'clock tonight. There, now: I've delivered the message. I don't think we'll meet again."

83

Alcan held out the statuette of Horus. Gorodish refused it with a small gesture of his left hand.

It was almost five in the afternoon when Alba finally woke. She dressed quickly and went downstairs to the dining room. Ludovic, as pleasant and as distant as ever brought her a glass of banana Nesquik, two sunny-side up eggs and a bowl of fruit salad. Ludovic rarely spoke to Alba, as if he was afraid he might like her.

Breakfast over, Alba went out into the courtyard. The R-16 was gone: Charley was off shopping. Alba decided to take a walk around the grounds. She did not bother putting on her jogging shorts.

Louis was probably in the living room, poring over his encyclopedia and drinking orange juice. Marco was undoubtedly upstairs, putting away his paints and cleaning his brushes.

Alba walked up the small beaten path to the kennels. She kneeled down and spoke quietly and affectionately to the dogs, as if she could bribe them into silence or ensure their complicity in her plans. Alba was no longer afraid of the animals. She pushed her hand through the chain link fence and petted their large, intimidating heads.

Alba continued her afternoon walk, suddenly deciding that it would do her good to run. She tried not to think about the escape, but her mind and her body were effervescent with anticipation.

Wanting a change from her usual itinerary, Alba headed toward the compost heap which, unfortunately, was situated well within the limits of her exercise area. She decided to run as far as the small barrier marking the boundary of the secured area when suddenly a small piece of waxed paper caught her eye. She picked it up.

For days now Alba had been searching for a clue to where

84

she was being held and now a wayward breeze had come to her aid. Quite obviously the paper had fallen from a garbage can. Printed in blue on the mottled, waxed background were the words:

Rilhac-Xaintrie Dairy Cooperative
Butter, milk, cheese.
Cantal (France)

Alba folded the paper carefully and slipped it under the elastic at the top of her panties. If she made good her escape from the château she might not need the paper, yet something told her to hold on to this precious piece of evidence.

She went back to the château, stole an envelope from the living-room desk, then went up to the attic room and put a Haydn sonata on the turntable, one of the sonatas that Gorodish loved to play.

Louis was in the attic room, pacing back and forth in front of the sheet-covered painting.

"Have you seen it?" he asked.

"Yes," Alba said coldly.

"Is it beautiful?"

"It's okay, I guess."

"I've told Charley and Ludovic to make a special dinner tonight."

"I'm sick of being a dragonfly," Alba whined, "I want to be a praying mantis."

"Of course. You can be any insect you like! We'll look through my entomological encyclopedia."

"Listen, is Charley going to stay here?"

"That's the plan. Why?"

"Oh, buu-um: you know why. I'm sort of getting used to you, but I'll never get used to him. Never. Do I have to dress up like a dragonfly tonight?"

"You may do whatever you like."

85

"For once." Alba said, putting another record on the turntable. She turned the volume down and said, "I want some new records."

"Make a list. Anything you like," Delaborde said expansively.

"Well, alert the media," Alba said sarcastically and turned up the volume again. Sitting down on the couch, she closed her eyes. Delaborde watched her hungrily, hoping that one day she would willingly take part in his harmless little games.

Alba could feel the waxed paper against her skin. This time it was difficult to lose herself in the music.

Delaborde had told Ludovic to set the table in the attic room, next to the portrait of Luna. Around nine in the evening Ludovic lit the candles and Delaborde began the festivities by opening two bottles of champagne. He had invited the entire household to the party, like a prince anxious to display his latest acquisition to his approving courtiers.

Ludovic did not look very comfortable in the society of his betters, but Charley had taken advantage of the occasion to dress himself entirely in white. He sat puffing on a cigar, making small talk with Louis.

One of Delaborde's insect tapes was running, taking the place of background music. The chirping, chittering sounds brought back unhappy memories to Alba.

With Marco's approval, Delaborde now removed the sheet to display the painting, his eyes beaming with perverse pleasure, his face set in the same expression as when he had first thrown himself on his sweet insect.

"Magnificent!" Delaborde exclaimed. "Absolutely extraordinary!" Charley and Ludovic stared at the portrait, Charley out of politeness, Ludovic out of curiosity.

86

Luna's magic body, dressed in her costume, stood in the foreground, gleaming under the moonlight. The red velvet couch seemed to melt into the background, transformed into a landscape, a sort of blood-red jungle that appeared to be swarming with a thousand strange, barely discernible insect forms. In the painting Alba's pure face, bathed in tears, resembled an eighteenth-century madonna.

Delaborde handed the artist a sealed envelope.

"It looks exactly like Mademoiselle Luna," Ludovic said.

Charley said nothing. The painter disgusted him, the portrait disgusted him. It was absolutely ridiculous wasting money on a painting of that bitch.

They sat down to dinner, Ludovic serving before joining them at the table. He would have preferred eating alone in the kitchen: that way he could have taken larger portions and seconds.

Alba ate, piling spoonfuls of caviar on toast triangles, sipping at her champagne. The others were hitting the vodka. She watched them drink. Later, in the middle of the meal, she got up and refilled their glasses. Often.

An automatic slide projector clicked steadily, displaying photographs of insects on a large screen. The painting stood on an easel, facing Louis across the table. He stared at it admiringly, avidly.

Despite the abundant food and the rarity of the wines, the atmosphere in the room was tense. Only Delaborde seemed to be enjoying himself.

"It's too bad that you have to go so soon," Delaborde said to Marco. "When are you leaving for Paris?"

"I'll need another three or four days before the painting is ready to be varnished, and then a few more days for it to dry. As soon as that's done, I'll be going. I'm afraid I've fallen behind schedule on my other work."

"That's too bad," Delaborde said, and then proceeded to

question Marco about the painter's craft, about how the gallery system worked, about the cost of canvas and paints.

Ludovic brought in fruit tarts and ices.

Alba tried not to look at Marco. Charley sat in a corner, smoking the Havana cigar that Delaborde had given him. Ludovic brought in a bottle of old Calvados and poured it into brandy snifters. He opened the skylight and the warm night air crept into the room.

Alba pretended interest in the conversation but her mind was elsewhere.

Around two in the morning, Ludovic excused himself and went to bed. After he left, time seemed to crawl. Finally, Charley disappeared. Alba's eyes flicked over his retreating figure, wondering if he had drunk enough to put him to sleep. Marco's head began to nod. Alba did not want to be alone with Delaborde. She rose quietly and went down to the ground floor. Charley's and Ludovic's bedroom windows were dark. She went back up to her own room, undressed, took a shower, put on her sweat suit and slipped into bed. Fearing that Delaborde might take it into his head to drop in on her, as he so often had, she turned off the light.

The quiet was broken only by the cries of night birds and the sound of her own heartbeat.

At last the door opened and a shadowy figure approached the bed. "Let's go," Marco said.

They ran down the stairs and into the courtyard. The cloud cover hiding the moon was gone and the night sky seemed lighter.

"Here's the wire," Marco whispered. "Twist the ends hard. I've taken care of the R-16. I'll be waiting in the car. Hurry."

He hugged Alba. She ran through the forest to the kennel. The dogs whined as she approached. Alba spoke to them in a whisper. The dogs trotted nearer, sniffing at her. She slipped the wire around the door and doorpost, twisted it tightly and spread the ends, bending them upward. The dogs watched as she walked away, then lay down again.

Marco was waiting behind the wheel as Alba got into the car. He buckled his seat belt.

"I'm going to try to break through the gate," he said. "You better protect your face."

He turned the ignition key. The station wagon was old. It took a good fifteen seconds for the engine to catch. The headlights blazed down the dirt driveway along the line of shadowy trees. Alba braced herself against the dashboard as the car sped away from the château.

Charley heard the car start. It took him no more than three seconds to reach the window and see the rear lights disappearing in the distance. He shouted, and Ludovic and Delaborde came running. Charley had already pulled on his trousers and a pair of moccasins. He grabbed his straight razor, picked up a loaded carbine, snatched up the keys to the R-16 . . . and the alarm went off.

Still in his pajamas, Ludovic slipped into a pair of shoes, picked up his .45 and ran down the stairs. Charley was trying to start the car.

"The bastard!" he shrieked as Ludovic came up behind him. "Come on!" Ludovic was already running up the road. Charley turned on the headlights. When Delaborde reached the courtyard he caught sight of Charley and Ludovic disappearing around a turn in the road. He was surprised to hear the dogs barking and ran to the kennel. It took him only a minute to discover the wire, and another long moment to untwist it.

Finally he managed to open the kennel door. The dogs headed for the woods. When Delaborde returned to the R-16, there was nothing left but an empty driveway.

89

* * *

The heavy gate loomed up in front of the station wagon. "Goddam!" Marco shouted, "it's a goddam fortress! We can't get through it. Undo your seat belt, Alba! I'm going to park next to the wall. Jump up on the car roof, go over the wall and run as fast as you can. I'll be right behind you."

Marco slammed on the brakes and turned the steering wheel sharply. The station wagon skidded sideways and smashed into the wall.

Marco charged out of the car, Alba right behind him. It took them mere seconds to clamber up onto the car roof.

"Shit! I forgot the lights!" Marco climbed down again, shouting "Jump, goddamit!" to Alba who was waiting for him on top of the wall. He turned off the headlights. The men following them would have less of a target to aim at.

Charley's heart felt as if it were going to burst as he tried to catch up with Ludovic. The older man was in better shape and had been trained for this sort of thing. The dogs had already passed both of them, gliding silently through the night.

Two shadows appeared. "Marco, the dogs!" Alba called. He did not even have a chance to reach the wall before one of the dogs seized him by the throat.

Ludovic could barely make out Alba standing on top of the wall. He crouched, aimed and emptied the gun in her direction.

At the first sound of gunfire, Alba jumped. A round whistled past her, the other bullets smashing into the wall or losing themselves in the forest. She heard Marco cry out, then nothing more. The edge of the forest was only sixty feet away. She heard one of the gunmen jump up onto the roof

90

of the car. Alba turned and ran toward the woods. She could see nothing in the dark and the ground was soft underfoot. It felt as if she was running through beds of ferns.

Marco's neck was broken. The dogs did not let go until the body stopped moving. Then they jumped over the wall.

Ludovic slapped another magazine into the .45. He could see nothing in the dark but heard someone running and fired in the direction of the sound before climbing over the wall. Still trying to catch up with Ludovic, Charley managed to drag himself up onto the wall.

"She isn't far," Ludovic shouted as he entered the woods.

The ground grew firmer underfoot as she crossed a clearing. She could hear the dogs coming through the ferns and stopped to face them. They were on her almost immediately. She spoke to them and the dogs stopped and crouched at her feet, tongues lolling, sides heaving. Alba bent over and petted them. She could hear heavier footsteps breaking through the fern beds now. She moved away slowly, the dogs staying where she had left them.

When she had moved far enough away from the dogs, she began to run again. It was harder going now. Brambles caught at her clothes and whipped at her face and hands. Desperately, Alba tried to see through the dark, moving onward with no idea of where she was going, lost in the night as she tried to put as much distance as she could between herself and her pursuers.

After a while the ground slanted downward and then became flat again. The forest around her seemed to lighten slightly and Alba realized she was on a path. She began to run as fast as she could, then, lengthening her stride even farther, faster.

CHAPTER

7

ALBA STOPPED TO CATCH HER
breath, listening intently to the strange sounds filling the
forest. At any moment now she expected to see Charley
come looming out of the dark, menacing underbrush. It was
too dangerous to stay on the path so she turned and headed
deeper into the woods, running blindly, stopping from time
to time to listen to the unidentifiable sounds before running
again. Her strength was ebbing. Her skin was torn by brambles and thorns and she could feel trickles of warm blood
running down her legs. She tripped and fell. The ground
was soft and aromatic, blanketed with twigs. She rose immediately and went on, afraid that she was running in circles,
driven by the dread of Charley's finding her.

It was only when she had run herself into exhaustion that
Alba stopped and dragged herself into a thicket, her senses
on the alert, her mind frozen with terror.

A bird chirped and suddenly the forest was alive with
birdsong. A little while later the sky grew lighter and dawn

began to filter through the trees. The forest seemed a little less terrifying now.

Alba dragged herself from the thicket, her clothes in shreds, her body aching. She began to walk again, listening, not knowing where she was going. She came to a large clearing and saw a line of beehives; crossing the clearing she moved on until she reached a meadow. A few cows stood grazing in the deep grass. Beyond the meadow was a village, several of the houses showing light through their windows. Alba was afraid to ask for refuge. She knew that the men would not give up their search but would comb the entire region to find her. Despite her fear, she decided it would be safer to remain in the forest.

The village consisted of a dozen houses. From her hiding place in the woods she could make out the small church and the town square. A yellow spot caught her eye: a mailbox. Alba remembered the waxed-paper wrapping. She reached inside her waistband and removed the crumpled, dirty paper: it was slightly the worse for wear. She had to reach Gorodish: he could be at the village in two days. She had no pen, no stamps. She wondered if the letter would be delivered even without stamps. Picking up a twig, she used her fingernails to peel away the thin cover of dried bark.

Through a rip in her sweat pants she tore away a scab and, dipping the point of the twig in her own blood, wrote Gorodish's name and address on the envelope. The blood took on a brownish hue as it dried. Alba examined the waxed-paper wrapping, then underlined the name of the village where the dairy cooperative was located. It occurred to her that she would be better off telling Gorodish where she was hiding now. Alba made her way through the woods, circling the village until she came upon a sign at the side of the road. She knelt down, dipped the twig in her own blood again and wrote:

93

*Hiding in forest near Arches. Come! Ran from château.
They're looking for me. Love, Alba.*

When the blood dried, Alba made her way over hedgerows, through stands of trees and behind barns until she reached a flat area near the mailbox. There was almost two hundred yards of open ground to cross and she prayed that nobody would see her. She stood absolutely still for a long moment, making sure the village street was empty, before crossing the road and running quickly to the box. She kissed the envelope before dropping it through the slot.

The dogs seemed to have lost the trail. Charley and Ludovic went on without them, searching for hours before finally admitting to themselves that the girl was really gone.

Returning to the château, they buried the painter's body and checked to see if his battered station wagon would still run. Ludovic found the distributor head inside the station wagon and replaced it in the R-16.

Delaborde was on the verge of collapse. It had never occurred to him that his disappearance might lead to someone's death. In hysterics, he ordered Charley and Ludovic to find Alba.

They set off in the two cars at dawn. None of the men had been able to figure out why the dogs had not killed Alba, too.

Delaborde rode with Charley. Ludovic rode alone. They were all armed.

André Leroy was mending an old barbed-wire fence when he saw something out of the corner of his eye. Leroy looked up, squinted slightly, and saw a dark figure, blond hair streaming, run quickly toward the forest. Leroy had just enough time to make out the figure's torn clothing when it disappeared.

Hey, he said to himself.

Leroy finished mending the fence and then went home to tell his wife and sons what he had seen. Despite the fact that André Leroy was neither an alcoholic nor subject to hallucinations, his family did not believe his story.

Alba stood at the edge of the woods, observing the village and the surrounding countryside. She had managed to mail the letter; now it was time to hide again, to go deeper into the forest.

Her legs ached and she was hungry, her throat dry and burning with thirst. She walked a few more miles, making mental note of landmarks so that she could find her way back to the village.

She came to a rutted path cut by tractor tires. Keeping out of sight, she followed the track up to an isolated farm. Two men were stacking wood under a lean-to. Geese and chickens ran between the farm buildings and a small herd of cattle moved slowly through the surrounding meadows.

A German shepherd lay chained to a large doghouse in front of the main building. Alba retreated up the path.

Two milk cans stood at the foot of the lane. Alba waited a moment, then, hearing nothing move, crept forward and opened one of the cans. It was full. She knelt, gripped the can by its handles and tilted it toward her. A thick, creamy, fragrant liquid soothed her feverish mouth and burning throat. In her haste she spilled some of the milk. It ran down her neck and onto her clothes, dripping to the ground where it formed a small, white puddle. After drinking her fill, Alba replaced the top on the milk can and moved back into the forest, heading toward the village in hopes of finding a safe hiding place.

The sun was high when Alba came upon a small, sandy-bottomed cave hidden behind a tangle of brambles and leaves. Carefully pushing aside the prickly shrubs, she managed to wriggle into the cave, pulling the bushes back into place behind her. She lay down on the cool, sandy floor.

It was only then that she thought of Marco. He had given up his life for her. Alba wept a long time, thinking of him, thinking of Gorodish. Gorodish would come soon, now. Gorodish would avenge Marco's death.

Alba fell asleep, curled up on the cave floor. When she woke it was night. Terror returned and she huddled inside the cave, barely breathing, her eyes searching the dark, imagining that she could hear steps approaching.

In the village café, André Leroy ordered a small glass of white wine and then carried it over to the large wood table in the center of the room. A dozen men sat around the table, discussing the day's events, their farms, the weather, politics, the upcoming cattle market day at Mauriac, the county seat.

"Has anybody seen gypsies around here lately?" Leroy asked.

"Why? Did someone steal your wife?" one of the farmers laughed.

"No. Nobody stole nothin' from me. This mornin' I was mendin' the fence over at Five Acres when I saw someone runnin' through the woods. A blond girl, dressed in rags."

"Maybe it was the Holy Virgin," a farmer suggested. "We'll write the bishop, tell him you had a religious vision. That oughta bring in the tourists. We'll be rich, have us a two-star restaurant an' a hotel for the nuns comin' in on pilgrimage."

"Don't joke, Roger. Maybe Leroy did see somebody. Somethin' got at my milk cans; there was a puddle of milk onna ground. I hadda get down off my tractor, take a good look, they was missin' maybe a couple of liters."

"A werewolf."

96

"Or a wild child, been brought up by the wild boars down in the Dordogne valley," Sébastien Lupot suggested. Lupot was slightly retarded, a loner, and not particularly liked by people in the surrounding villages. He lived like an animal gone to earth on a miserable farm far from the village. His farmhouse was a hovel set on the bank of a large creek that fed into the Dordogne River. Lupot shared the farm with his idiot brother, Antoine, and their aged mother who had spent the last ten years of her life sitting paralyzed in a battered wheelchair.

The Lupot brothers survived by poaching: they knew the forest better than anyone else in the area. They raised a few chickens and grew a few vegetables on a small plot of land near their ramshackle barn. They never had visitors. From time to time, when they had some money, the brothers would come into the village and get drunk.

Nobody knew where they got their money. One time they had paid for a drink with an old gold piece, leading to rumors that the old woman had a hidden treasure buried somewhere on the property. The brothers and their mother lived in one room. The hovel had not been cleaned since the day, ten years earlier, when the old woman had suddenly lost the use of her legs. The Lupot brothers were filthy, their hair crawling with vermin. Sébastien's face was tiny, wizened, as wrinkled as a dried apple, and he had a cast in one eye. Antoine had never been able to speak properly and could only grunt whenever he had something to say. Only Sébastien and his mother could understand him. The brothers owned a mangy, one-eyed dog named Ratto.

"My brother says we oughta organize a hunt, beat the woods for the Gypsy girl."

"Good idea. Only it's not a girl, it's an animal."

It was four in the morning when the Lupot brothers finally returned home, falling-down drunk. They had forgot-

97

ten to move their mother inside; she had slept out on the porch all night and was soaked through with the night dew. A layer of smoke hung over the countryside, rising from the warm earth into the silvery morning air. The brothers lifted the old woman and carried her inside. She did not wake. Day was breaking. The brothers fell on their pallets and immediately began to snore.

CHAPTER

8

The INTERCOM BUZZED.

"Who is it?" Gorodish asked.

"The postman, monsieur. I have a letter here, postage due."

"Just a minute. I'll be right down."

Too impatient to wait for the elevator, Gorodish ran down the stairs, crossed the entry hall and snatched the letter from the postman's hand. A ten-franc note quickly soothed the man's indignation.

"Keep the change," Gorodish said, running toward the elevator. He had recognized Alba's handwriting and had seen that the address was written in blood.

He leaned against the elevator wall, his strength sapped by the violence of the emotions running through him, as he opened the envelope, took out the paper and read the message.

Back in his apartment he found a map of France, glanced at it and immediately realized it would be far more efficient to find out exactly where the village was located. He dialed Information, then went to a cupboard and took out a map of the province of Auvergne. He found the village almost immediately.

Gorodish looked at his watch. It was five-forty in the afternoon. Alba, his blond angel, was alive; Alcan, as hostage, would ensure she remained that way. It would take about eight hours to drive to the village. He gathered his identity papers, some money, the key to his country house and his .45 automatic. Then he left the apartment.

Alcan was extremely nervous about the meeting and arrived at the shopping mall a half hour early. He took advantage of the extra time to flirt with the bookstore manager: she was not displaying his books properly. It suddenly occurred to him that he might want a souvenir of the historic occasion and hurried to buy a Polaroid camera. Then he returned to wait in front of the bookstore, checking his watch anxiously every few minutes.

A strange creature came through the glass doors into the shopping mall. It was wearing a raincoat and a black *papier-mâché* falcon's head over its face.

Alcan instantly sensed the subtle meaning of the symbolism. He snapped a picture, wondering if Freud still wore a beard. Horus drew nearer. Alcan knew that this was a moment that would go down in history: the first meeting between two demigods: The Father, The Son. . . . He trembled, feeling like a boy about to lose his virginity.

Two bright eyes peered at him from beneath the mask. Freud kissed Alcan on both cheeks, then began to speak in Viennese-accented French.

"Glad to meet you," said Freud.

"Me, too."

"Let's take a walk. . . . Would you like a cigar?"

100

"No, thank you. But please smoke, if you like."

Gorodish/Horus/Freud lit a Havana cigar and stuck it into a hole in his beak.

"I bet you never expected anything like this, did you, Alcan?"

"I must admit I was taken aback when your messenger showed up, but then I realized he had no appointment, and it was between three and four in the afternoon, the hour when you used to receive patients in Vienna, and I remembered that you never actually made appointments . . . but I was somewhat troubled by his . . ."

"Have you read the Talmud?"

"No."

"That probably explains a certain lack of backbone that I sense in you. Of course I admit that your analytic ramblings are absolutely brilliant, but still . . ."

"Please elucidate," Alcan said tensely. It had been a long time since he had had to explain his actions.

Freud walked very briskly. Alcan was out of breath. Children laughed as they passed.

"First of all, it seems to me that the remarkably open manner in which you speak to your students and which, I must add, I admire, was directly influenced by the teaching techniques of my own professor, Dr. Charcot. Your lecture style is to some extent a 'replay' of his famous Tuesday-afternoon classes."

"True, but . . ."

"Good. I thought that point needed clearing up. I should also like to mention a certain number of irreverent remarks about me that you . . ."

"Are we not expected to rebel against The Father?"

"Yes. But there are limits. For example, I do not appreciate your attitude toward my most brilliant pupil, my youngest protégée. You can't begin to know the trouble I went to,

101

from the Beyond, to make certain your paths crossed. And your theories on silence in therapy are in direct contradiction to everything I ever . . ."

"You mean that little blond girl . . ."

"Yes. I have come back to earth to save her. And I consider your recent behavior a serious lapse in our deontology. . . ."

Alcan was shaking. Freud kept walking.

". . . therefore, in atonement, you must dissolve the movement you have created in my name. . . ."

"Oh, I want to atone. . . ."

"Good," Freud said, patting him on the shoulder. "The girl is a repository of important information. In fact, she knows everything I have learned since my death. . . ."

"But there was nothing about her to indicate, no visible sign . . ."

"Her beauty was the visible sign of her perfect wisdom." Alcan had become extremely agitated. Freud deliberately ignored the man's fatigue and even stepped up the pace each time Alcan tried to slow down.

"We must leave immediately," Alcan said. "I don't know what that crazy bug might do to her."

"Her name alone, so immaculately conceived, so symbolic of the rebirth of light, of wisdom, should have told you, Jacques."

Alcan beamed. Freud had used his first name. Maybe Freud's affection and forgiveness were not lost to him.

"I'll take care of the movement when I get back," Alcan said. "I promise you that every single one of my followers will bend to your wishes."

"I better not have wasted my time for nothing," Freud warned. "My car's outside in the parking lot. I'll drive. You talk."

* * *

102

Armed with rifles and accompanied by their hunting dogs, a dozen men gathered in the village square. They deployed themselves in a long skirmish line and moved toward the woods. Alba realized that they were looking for her. Not waiting to see any more, she ran toward the large creek she had discovered deep within the forest.

The dogs raced ahead of the hunting party, the men following more slowly. Antoine and Sébastien Lupot were in the middle of the line. They were hung over, but they would not have missed the hunt for anything in the world.

At his country house, Gorodish picked up his Remington 12-gauge shotgun and loaded a cartridge belt with buckshot. He had bought the Remington in Belgium during one of his many trips there.

He drove through Vierzon and crossed the province of Berry. Alcan sat in the backseat, bound hand and foot.

Rain clouds filled the sky and the country roads were almost deserted. Around ten in the evening Gorodish reached Saint-Août. Its streets were empty and a fierce wind blew bits of trash along the sidewalks.

The night was black but Gorodish drove on. A small titmouse hit the windshield and exploded. Glancing in the rearview mirror, Gorodish saw its remains lying on the sleet-slick road. In the meadows on either side of the road, large white Charolais cattle cropped grass in the deepening gloom.

Gorodish drove past George Sand's home at Nohant and turned onto a county road leading toward Guéret. His eyes never left the two-lane highway glistening yellow in the glare of his headlights. The rain beat down. Gorodish slowed the car.

At Sainte-Feyre he caught sight of a hillside covered with cemetery crypts, pointed roofs rising upward, the hill resem-

103

bling a small sleeping village. He shuddered at the overwhelming impression of death and desolation. A shabby circus stood in the village square. A pony watched him pass by, its eyes pus-filled and sad.

At Lavey-les-Mines, Gorodish saw a garden filled with rosebushes pruned so the red flowers formed a heart. A drunk zigzagged down the middle of the road on a bicycle. Gorodish pumped the brakes lightly and passed the man, then pressed down on the accelerator again. Alcan was asleep.

Piles of firewood lay at the edge of the forest. Gorodish chided himself for not having brought his paints and brushes. They would have been camouflage, would have helped explain his interest in the area. He turned on the car radio and listened to the last movement of Schumann's Fourth Symphony.

The city of Limoges lay quiet, its streets and roads empty. He entered the province of Creuse and found only empty, abandoned villages. A worm-eaten blue sign hung in front of a house, naming it, describing it: SOLITUDE.

The road seemed more and more desolate and he passed fewer villages now. Suddenly an animal seemed to throw itself in front of the car. Gorodish did not have time to brake. He felt a heavy shock against the wheels. Probably a dog. Probably dead. The road began to climb, winding upward in a series of hairpin turns before opening out onto the Plateau de Millevaches. The road ran straighter now, bordered on both sides by petrified, moss-covered trees the color of mildew. Gorodish felt very alone, lost in the immense emptiness of a funereal, hostile Nature.

Enormous raindrops pelted the windshield, exploding as they hit. At long last the rain stopped. The land looked as if it had been washed clean. The sky turned dark blue and the stars appeared.

104

*   *   *

Frustrated, feeling as if they had been chasing a ghost, the farmers finally abandoned the hunt. Only the Lupot brothers went on. Expert poachers, they had spotted tracks and the telltale signs of someone moving through the forest. Now they were alone in the night, their rifles at the ready, accompanied only by their mangy, one-eyed dog.

Alba's strength was gone. The deeper she moved into the woods the more she felt that she was entering an area of desolation. It was as if Nature were playing with her, forcing her to stumble over fallen trees and roots, deliberately hurting her. The night seemed to have penetrated her body and taken possession of her belly, her head, her eyes. From time to time she thought she heard a dog barking and the sound of voices coming toward her, the sounds distorted by the woods and by distance. Each time she fell, only the dread in her soul kept her going.

Gorodish stopped to check the map. It was after two in the morning. In the backseat, Alcan awakened. "Are we there yet, boss?"

"Not yet. What happens if she manages to get away?"

"Then we'll have to worry about Charley."

"Who's that?"

"A mercenary I hired for the job. He's a sadist."

Gorodish pulled Alcan out of the car. He led him deep into the forest and pushed him to the ground underneath an oak tree.

"Jacques, if you move from this spot, you're a dead man."

"I won't move, boss."

"If I don't find Alba I'll tear your heart out with my beak."

"I'll do anything you want, boss; let me come with you," Alcan begged.

105

"Don't you move," said Horus, and left Alcan alone in the dark.

Exhausted, Antoine and Sébastien Lupot kept searching, sure that they were on the right trail.

"She's heading upstream, off the big river," Sébastien said. "We've got her now."

Antoine moaned and gurgled his agreement.

Alba could hear the muffled sound of the current and headed toward the bank of the dark, broad creek. It was only when she reached the water's edge that she realized she was trapped. Exhausted, she slipped to the ground. A few minutes later she heard sounds and a deep voice urging a dog on. She felt the dog's muzzle on her neck. The dog barked. She heard steps.

Two shadows loomed over her and she tried to get up, but a rifle barrel forced her flat to the damp ground. Two men knelt down and peered at her. When she saw their faces, Alba screamed.

"It's a devil. Leroy was right. But we're not gonna tell we found her, Antoine."

An animal noise came from the other man. Alba did not even have the strength to scream again.

"Mama's gonna be happy," Sébastien said, pulling Alba up by her hair. "Strike a match; let's see what it looks like."

The faint light illuminated the faces of the monstrous beings bending over her: two brutish idiots, teeth missing from their vacant grins, eyes as dull as death, their expressions avid.

"We're gonna keep her inna barn. We got us a woman now."

Alba fainted. Antoine, the stronger of the two brothers, hoisted her to his shoulder and let out another animal cry.

"Thass right," Sébastien said; "we're goin home."

Slowly, heavily, they made their way upstream.

106

Gorodish turned on the car radio. A piano was playing the "Funeral March" from Chopin's Second Piano Sonata. Gorodish shivered: for a moment it seemed like a bad omen. Ten minutes later he drove into the village square at Arches where Alba had said she would meet him.

Crossing the square he drove up a narrow road leading into the forest. A sign told him he was heading toward the hamlet of Le Cheix. Halfway there he stopped and turned off the radio.

He scanned the edge of the woods, half expecting to see Alba step out into the open and walk toward him. He did not sound the car horn for fear of attracting attention. Gorodish tried to see past the curtain of foliage at the edge of the woods. Time passed. The pain in his heart grew sharper.

He wanted to cry out, to call her name, but intuition told him that Alba was not there. Maybe *they* had caught up with her.

Going back to the car, he checked the shotgun, loaded another magazine for the .45 automatic and turned on the radio again. He tried to make his mind a blank as the heart-rending voice of Maria Callas sang the death aria from *Norma*, but, unable to bear it any longer, Gorodish finally switched off the radio.

He could not decide what to do next. Alba had said she would meet him here and he knew that she would do everything in her power to keep her promise. If she could. But if she was being held by someone, Gorodish was losing precious time. He tried to convince himself that Alba had simply fallen asleep, or that she had become lost during the night, but he was trembling, his heart telling him that she was hurt.

A man came out of a house that hugged the bottom of the road, looked up toward Gorodish and then slowly

107

walked toward him. Gorodish hid the shotgun and the .45.

"Mornin'," the man said.

"Good morning," Gorodish replied, forcing himself to smile. The man looked back over his shoulder.

"You lookin' for the wild girl?"

"What wild girl?"

"Yesterday mornin' somebody thought he saw a girl runnin' inna woods. She had blond hair, he said, an' we been havin' some robberies aroun' here, so we organized a hunt. Too bad, though; we didn' find nothin'. People around here say maybe she's a child been abandoned by Gypsies. Some of 'em think she's one of them children raised up by wild animals. I heard of that happenin'. She runs so fast, maybe she *was* raised up by animals. They say she's dressed in rags. Maybe she didn't get so far away; you be careful you lock your car."

"I don't have anything of value with me," Gorodish said. "Is there a café near here?"

"Down inna village."

"If you see her, or hear someone talking about her, I'd like to know about it."

Gorodish shook hands with the farmer, then he got back in the car and drove down to the village. He went into the café, hoping to hear more gossip about the wild child. If there had been a hunt, Alba would have fled as far as possible from her pursuers.

He sat down in a corner and ordered a cup of coffee and a sandwich. Five men sat at a table, drinking from a bottle of rum and talking about the hunt and the wild child.

Gorodish stayed in the café long enough to learn that the Lupot brothers were still searching and that they had not been seen in the village since the night before.

Not wanting to arouse the farmers' curiosity, Gorodish did not ask where the Lupot brothers lived but left the café, went back to his car and drove out of the village, heading toward the forest where Alba was supposed to meet him.

He reached the two dilapidated houses that made up the hamlet of Le Cheix. A woman was hanging out laundry and Gorodish stopped to ask her where the Lupot brothers lived.

"Scum," the woman answered, adding: "You don't want to go near them. Poachers. Live in a pigsty near the creek. Place called La Lirande."

Gorodish thanked her and found the Lupot property on the map. The farm was set in a bend of a large creek that fed into the Dordogne River. There was no road leading to the house, but there appeared to be a path running along the bank on the far side of the creek. Gorodish decided to go take a look.

CHAPTER

9

ALBA WOKE TO FIND HERSELF INside a barn, her ankles and wrists bound and tied to two beams. Her entire body was sore and there was not enough play in the rope to allow her to move. She lay on a pile of straw. Chickens roosted nearby and the barn stank of animal droppings. Daylight streamed in past the top of the half-open door and through a few broken roof tiles.

Alba remembered the two bestial faces bending over her, the hunt, the dogs, the mad race through the forest, the dark creek.

She was a prisoner again. Outside, she could hear chickens cackling and the sound of running water. Someone was sawing wood. Slowly, she could feel her courage returning. She stared at the ropes binding her, hoping to free herself, but they were too tight, too well knotted. Alba was tempted to scream, but knew it would serve no purpose.

A while later she heard voices, and then steps approaching. The barn door opened and the Lupot brothers came in. Alba tugged frantically at the ropes, trying to break them, but they only tightened further around her wrists and ankles. Sébastien kneeled down next to her and grabbed her by the hair.

"All right, liddle bitch, you been stealin' from the farmers. . . ." Alba was too frightened to answer him.

"You're a Gypsy, ain't you?"

Alba burst into tears.

"You don' fool us, so you stop pretendin'. You thought you could get away from us but we know the woods real good. We caught you, didn' we, hunh?"

Antoine squealed and grunted.

"My brother says you're like him," Sébastien said. "He says you can't talk."

Alba could not answer him: the words would not come.

"You belong to us now, an' you're gonna pay. You're not bad lookin', hunh? An' you're young, you're strong. Mama, she's been sittin' in tha' damn chair, not doin' nothin', anna two of us, hell, we ain' had a woman inna long time. You're gonna do Mama's work, an' then you're gonna do tha' thing for me an' my brother." Sébastien began to laugh.

Antoine crept closer, abandoning his rifle on a pile of straw to crawl toward Alba, squealing as he came.

Sébastien translated: "He wantsa see how you're built."

The men were filthy, dirt so deeply embedded in their skin that they looked the color of soil. Alba cried out as Sébastien pulled the bottom of her sweat shirt up over her face. The two idiots began feeling her belly, pinching her breasts with their rough, heavy hands. They ripped away what was left of her pants and underwear, laughing, grunting, Antoine screeching, the sounds gasping and drawn out.

"He thinks you're pretty. He wants to keep you ou' here inna barn alla time; gonna fuck hisself silly. But he better leave some for me; I been waitin' long as him an' I'm not waitin' no longer."

The brothers undid the rope binding her legs together.

111

Antoine slipped another rope around one of her ankles; Sébastien did the same to the other leg.

Alba prayed that she would faint, but she did not. She remained conscious, her screams seeming to have no effect on the men. They pulled Alba's legs open, stretching the ropes taut and tying them to the barn poles. She suddenly thought that she had not brushed her teeth in several days, and she knew she would never see Gorodish again.

Inhuman sounds came from Antoine's mouth as he lay down on top of her. At that moment a shrill scream came from outside the barn. Antoine hesitated, leaned back on his heels, then rose, closed his pants and glared at his brother with a deadly look in his eye.

"Mama wantsa see you. We'll fuck you later."

They untied Alba, handed her the torn pants, pulled the sweat shirt back down around her waist and undid the rope holding her wrists.

"Get up, liddle bitch."

Alba got up, her legs aching. Sébastien tugged at the rope and they moved out of the barn. It was a beautiful morning. Alba could see the dark creek with its silvery reflections, its green-tinged water meandering through the forest. There were no other houses in sight, no other sign of life.

They walked up to the house. The old woman was sitting in the broken, rattan-backed wheelchair, clothed in bleached-out rags, her head almost bald, toothless, her lips barely visible, her face a parchment-covered skull. Her eyes were light-colored, cruel and staring. Her hands, deformed by arthritis, clutched the armrests; they looked like chicken feet.

"Is it the thief?" the mother asked, her words almost incomprehensible.

"Yes, Mama," Sébastien said.

"Why she yelling?"

112

"She like a animal, Mama."

"You been beatin' her?"

"No, we didn' do nothin' to her."

"You don' beat her too much, she work better."

"We won' hurt her, Mama."

"We still got that goat chain?"

"Inna barn."

"You go get it, chain her up, that way she can work but she can' run away. You get her a pair of pants, too."

"I'll go find somethin'," Sébastien said, and went into the house.

Alba looked at the black hole of the open door, unable to see into the house. Antoine sidled over to his mother and groaned a long question.

"No, boy," his mother said, "I don' wantchu makin' any babies. You better off dyin', leavin' nothing behind. An' the two of you'd get to fightin' over it, an' maybe killin' each other over it, an' then I'd be all alone here. You don' touch her, you hear me? Leave her alone, boy. There's never been a woman here for that, and there never's gonna be one. That thing," the old woman said, pointing at Alba, "that's nothin' but a work animal, an' don't you forget it."

Antoine began to shriek, pounding his fists furiously against his head before turning and running off into the woods.

Sébastien came hurrying from the house, carrying a pair of trousers. He looked at the old woman with hatred in his eyes. "Why you tell him that? He gonna have a fit, you know how he does, an' nex' time, he's gonna kill you, he's gonna wring your neck."

The old woman grinned and did not answer.

Sébastien handed Alba the pants. They were too large for her. He tied them around her waist with a length of string.

113

"She can do the dishes. They ain' seen soap an' water for a week or more."

"You put that chain on her first," the old woman said. "An' keep your eye on her."

Gorodish left his car far enough from the Lupot brothers' house so that it would not be seen. He took his binoculars, the map and his .45, leaving the shotgun in the car.

It took him twenty minutes, following the creek bank, to reach the small, bare sandspit on which the house sat.

He examined the buildings, the barn and the rabbit hutches, moving quietly, trying to get as close as possible without being seen, searching for a vantage point from which he could study the house and its surroundings at his leisure.

After having covered the entire region with no results, Charley and Ludovic finally ran across someone who told them the story of the wild girl, the hunt and the Lupot brothers. Someone else showed them where to find the small path that led to the isolated farm. They returned to the château to report to Delaborde what they had learned. He ordered them to follow up on the new trail while he remained at the château: poachers were touchy; you never knew what could happen. Charley and Ludovic returned to the forest path. Leaving their car at the edge of the woods they took their weapons and headed for the farm.

Pushing aside some branches for a clearer view, Gorodish studied the farm. A small dock lay in front of the house; a boat was tied up to it. Gorodish raised the binoculars and slowly panned the creek bank. A figure on the porch drew his attention. Adjusting the lenses he could make out the mummified figure of the old woman seated in her wheelchair.

*   *   *

A stake was planted in the ground halfway between the house and the barn. A chain hung from the stake. A dog paced back and forth inside a chain link fence lean-to, next to the rabbit hutches.

A man came out of the house. He was carrying a bowl that seemed to be filled with bread and milk. The man went to the barn, opened the door and disappeared inside. A moment later he reappeared and went back to the house. The old woman sat absolutely still, staring at the water.

The bowl had been too small to feed an animal. Maybe Alba was being kept prisoner in the barn. Gorodish realized he would have to cross the creek and find some way into the building. He remembered having seen a boat anchored near the car. Gorodish put away the binoculars, returned to the car and retrieved his shotgun.

Climbing down to the creek, Gorodish placed the shotgun and cartridge belt in the bottom of the boat, slipped the line, unshipped the oars and let the boat drift awhile before beginning to row. The current was stronger than it looked. He crossed the creek, rowing upstream, trying to make as little sound as possible.

He finally beached the boat on the far bank and reviewed what he knew of the farm. There were about one hundred yards of open meadow to cross, but he would be hidden by the barn.

Gorodish loaded five rounds of buckshot into the shotgun, looped the cartridge belt over his shoulder and tried to tell himself that he looked like a Mexican revolutionary in a movie. The terror and anxiety that had filled him since Alba's disappearance began to fade. His mind cleared and he could feel the adrenaline begin to flow through his body.

Gorodish moved forward, stopping every few steps to listen. He reached the edge of the woods and found himself above the barn and house. Just as he was about to step

115

forward, he heard a branch crack. A few seconds later a man holding a rifle walked out of the forest about fifty yards to Gorodish's right. The man was tall and dressed in rags. He hesitated for a moment, then walked determinedly toward the house, his rifle aimed at the door.

The old woman caught sight of him and cried out. Almost immediately Sébastien appeared in the doorway. At first he thought Antoine was pointing the rifle at the old woman. Then, from the crazy expression on his brother's face, Sébastien understood that the rifle was aimed at him.

He stood frozen, the old woman watching, not saying a word. Antoine took a few steps forward and began to yelp. Only the old woman and Sébastien understood what he was saying: "There's too many of us here. I want her for myself."

"You asshole," Sébastien shouted, "you're gonna wind up in prison, then you'll never have her. Put down the rifle! You wan' her so much, you can have her."

The old woman chimed in: "Put down the rifle, boy; you can have the girl. Your brother won't touch her, I'll see to that. You go ahead, do whatever you want with her, boy."

Slowly, Antoine shook his head. Then he pulled the trigger.

The blast lifted Sébastien, throwing him back into the house, his legs lying across the threshold. Antoine put down his rifle and walked over to make sure his brother was dead. He came out of the house again, went over to his mother and picked up the wheelchair.

"Put me down!" the old woman shrieked. "We'll be just fine now, the two of us. You did right, killin' him; he was no good."

Antoine yapped something at her. His mother seemed to understand what he was saying and fell silent. Antoine was having one of his fits, just as Sébastien had predicted. All this trouble for a bitch they'd found in the woods.

116

Carrying the wheelchair, Antoine walked toward the creek, went out onto the dock and stood looking down at the water.

The man's back was to him. Gorodish took advantage of the situation and headed for the barn. The dog began to bark but Antoine did not seem to hear him.

Gorodish glanced back toward the dock. Antoine was still standing there, holding the chair out over the water. The old woman sat absolutely still, looking into her son's face.

Antoine grunted, and threw the chair as far as he could. It hit the water. Antoine watched as his mother disappeared beneath the surface of the creek. He remained standing on the dock, peering at the water for several long minutes. At last the sound of the dog barking broke through his concentration. Antoine turned and dropped to the ground, as if he could smell danger. He wriggled toward his rifle, grabbed it and then ran to free the dog.

Gorodish aimed his shotgun directly at Antoine. He was about to pull the trigger when the dog yelped, turned and raced toward the woods.

CHAPTER

10

ANTOINE RAN TO THE RABBIT hutches and hid behind them. From somewhere deep in the woods the dog barked one more time; then there was silence. Gorodish could not reach the barn door: it was directly in Antoine's line of sight. Instead, he pressed back against the wall of the barn and stared into the forest. Nothing happened for at least ten minutes.

Ludovic moved out of the swaying mass of green at the forest's edge. One look at him and Gorodish knew the man was a professional. Ludovic took cover behind a rock. Gorodish was surprised that Antoine had not fired: he was probably waiting for a clear shot.

Ludovic peered out from behind the rock. Everything seemed quiet enough. Then he saw the two legs sticking out of the doorway and realized what the shot had been. The killer was probably still around somewhere, near the house. Ludovic waited a fairly long time, listening carefully, then ran toward a fallen tree and took cover behind it. Gorodish saw that the man was carrying a .45.

Another man came out of the forest to take cover behind the rock. Antoine still had not moved, waiting, with a poacher's patience, for the right moment.

Gorodish recognized the blond man as the one who had kidnapped Alba. There could be only one reason why the two men were here: Alba was in the barn.

Ludovic dropped to his belly and crawled through the high grass. Gorodish followed his progress as Ludovic snaked his way toward the house. Recognizing the animal instinct in Antoine, Gorodish decided to let him do the job.

Charley dashed across the clearing, hunched low and zig-zagging as he moved. Still, there was no reaction from Antoine. Ludovic was barely a dozen yards from the rabbit hutch now. Charley aimed his rifle at the house, covering Ludovic.

Ludovic knelt, his .45 aimed at the door. He resembled a round, compact ball with an automatic growing from it; or the biologic sign for the male gender. Carefully, he began to move toward the house.

Antoine fired twice, his body exposed only for the short time it took him to squeeze off two rounds. The third shot came from Charley's weapon.

Holding his belly, Ludovic collapsed. Antoine was wounded but he held absolutely still for a long moment before trying to retrieve his rifle. He began crawling back toward the rabbit hutches. Charley fired again. Antoine lay still. He looked dead.

Charley came out from behind the rock and, his gun still aimed at the body, walked toward Antoine. Charley turned his head to check on Ludovic. At that moment the poacher, in a last, dying effort, pulled the trigger. Charley screamed and grabbed his leg. Antoine died.

Gorodish could have finished Charley right then, but he decided to wait. Charley managed to grab hold of his rifle and dragged himself toward the barn.

119

He had a hard time opening the barn door. Alba stood at the back of the barn, tied to the beams. Charley dropped his rifle and pulled out his straight razor.

Alba stood between two posts, watching Charley drag himself toward her, a trail of blood marking his path. Gorodish had his finger on the trigger of the shotgun.

"You remember what I said I'd do," Charley shouted, brandishing the razor.

Alba seemed completely unmoved. There was no fear in her face. Gorodish was so shaken by the sight of her that he began to tremble, tears pouring down his face.

Then Alba spread her arms and Charley saw that she was no longer attached to the beams. She looked down at him, her expression as cold and empty as ever, watching him move toward her. A few feet more. Then Alba pulled a pitchfork from a bale of hay, walked toward Charley and with one terrible, ferocious thrust slammed the tines into his gut. The pitchfork passed through his body and pinned him to the ground.

Gorodish ran toward her, stopping when he saw Alba begin to wrestle the pitchfork from Charley's body and turn the tines toward him. He began to speak quietly as he slowly backed toward the barn door.

"Alba, it's all over. I'm here. It's me, it's Serge. Alba, my love, speak to me, say something. Put down the pitchfork, Alba. It's me. It's Serge."

She did not answer him but continued moving forward, Gorodish backing away, keeping a safe distance between them.

"It's all over, Alba. I've come to take you home. We're going back to Paris. Put down the pitchfork, Alba, let me hold you."

Alba's eyes were empty. She walked out of the barn, saw Antoine's body, went over to it and began stabbing the corpse, slamming the pitchfork viciously into the dead

120

man's back. Then she noticed Sébastien laying across the threshold, went over to the doorway and stabbed him over and over again. When she was finished, she began searching for something or somebody. Gorodish could not understand why she did not touch Ludovic's body, but realized that Alba was looking for the old woman, not knowing that the current had carried the harridan away.

He followed Alba around the farmyard, taking advantage of a moment's inattention to disarm her. Alba did not react. Gorodish took her face in his hands and looked into her eyes. Alba stared back at him, no recognition in her face. Gorodish repeated her name over and over again, trying to explain to her that it was all over, that nothing could harm her. She did not seem to hear him. Gorodish hugged her tightly. Alba stood there, not responding to his embrace.

"We're going home now," Gorodish said, leading Alba toward the boat. But the nymph resisted him, and Gorodish saw that she wanted the pitchfork. Gorodish gave it back to her, hoping that since she had not touched Ludovic's body, she would not harm him. He placed the pitchfork in the bottom of the boat, holding it down with one foot as he began to row. Alba sat facing him, looking off into the distance as if Gorodish did not exist. It took fifteen minutes of hard rowing to reach the car.

Gorodish helped Alba into the car. She insisted on holding the pitchfork and he let her; she still had not uttered a word.

They drove up a dirt road running through the forest. Alba became agitated as they neared the château. They came to a wall, its heavy iron gate standing open. Gorodish pulled out his .45 and placed it on the seat, then he took the shotgun from the back of the car and stood it between his knees. The château appeared at the end of the driveway.

121

*   *   *

Delaborde had been very nervous after Alba's escape but now he was much calmer. He was certain that she would return, certain that Charley and Ludovic would bring her back. He had told Charley not to hurt her: he wanted his dragonfly in one piece. But he would certainly have to punish her, make sure that she never ran away again. And he would never allow another outsider to enter his domain.

Delaborde waited impatiently, sitting in the attic room next to the portrait. It made him feel closer to his dragonfly. He put on one of the Haydn piano sonatas, took a cigar from the humidor, poured himself a glass of Armagnac and settled back to listen to the music.

There was a cleared area in the woods to the left of the driveway. Gorodish parked, took his shotgun and got out of the car. Alba did not wait for him but picked up the pitchfork and ran quickly toward the château, moving directly up the center of the driveway, like a knight in armor charging the enemy.

Gorodish could not catch her. He watched the blond hair streaming as she moved swiftly toward the château.

Alba crossed the courtyard at a dead run. The effort of opening the massive front door slowed her somewhat but she could hear music coming from the attic room and raced up the stairs, taking them two at a time. Gorodish followed her as best he could, still unable to catch up with her.

Alba opened the door to the attic room and saw Delaborde. She walked over to him, the pitchfork aimed straight at his heart. Delaborde was startled by the sound of the door opening, then he saw Alba and was overjoyed that his dragonfly had returned to him. A man appeared, standing behind his muse.

122

It was only then that Delaborde noticed the pitchfork and the shotgun. Terror filled him.

"No, don't do it. I'll make it up to you. I'm rich, very rich!"

Her eyes empty of all expression, Alba moved toward him. Delaborde could read his own death in her expression. "No," he said at the very moment his dragonfly planted the pitchfork in his belly, thrusting it through his body with every ounce of strength at her command. Gorodish pulled the trigger. Delaborde's body shuddered and fell to the floor.

Alba walked over to the turntable, turned off the stereo, took the record and slipped it neatly back into its sleeve. Then she went down into what had been her bedroom. Gorodish saw Marco's painting hanging against the attic wall. That vision of his angel, enmeshed in the devilish insect costume, made him shudder.

Gorodish went down the stairs and found Alba sitting on her bed. He took her in his arms but she did not react. Opening the closet doors, he began to erase every trace of her presence in the château. He found some large plastic bags and filled them with everything she might have touched or worn. Taking Alba by the hand, he gave her two of the plastic bags to carry and went back into the attic room.

An Oriental knife that had served as a paper cutter lay on the table. Gorodish cut the painting from the frame, rolled it, put it under his arm and dragged his mute angel down the stairs and out of the château.

He pushed her into the car, put the shotgun in the back seat and got in behind the wheel, pushing the .45 into his belt.

Alba opened the car door again and tore off the pants she had been given by Sébastien Lupot. Gorodish saw her bat-

123

tered legs. Alba searched through the plastic bags until she found a pair of jeans, shoes and a fresh blouse. Then she got into the car again and sat down next to Gorodish.

He picked up the discarded clothing, rolled the torn garments into a ball which he threw into the trunk of the car. He was determined that they leave nothing behind . . . except the dead man.

Gorodish drove quickly. They passed through Spontour and headed in the direction of Tulle and then on, through Egletons, Meymac and across the Plateau de Millevaches. The road was empty, almost deserted. From time to time, Gorodish pressed Alba's hand and looked over at her, hoping for a sign of life; but the nymph's expression remained dead.

His happiness at finding her was mixed with pain. Intuitively, he understood the terrible ordeal she had undergone.

Alba seemed emptied of all personality, all substance. He wondered how long that emptiness would last, how long it would be before she spoke again. She seemed to be nothing more than a body, bereft of soul, of feeling, of intelligence. The terrible emptiness began to affect him, too, spreading through his soul, and he spoke to Alba, trying to reach her, trying to strike a spark of recognition within her. To no avail.

"Alba, it's Serge. They're all dead. We're going home. It's over. We're together again. Nothing will ever separate us. I'll take care of you. You'll forget that nightmare. We'll be happy again."

Gorodish decided they would not return to Paris but instead would spend a few weeks at the country house. He thought it would make Alba's reentry into the world that much easier. They drove for several hours. Gorodish saw

124

that Alba was becoming sleepy. Her head fell forward several times, only to jerk up again. He pulled over to the side of the road and helped her into the backseat, making a pillow out of clothing, wrapping her in a blanket he kept in the car. She fell asleep almost immediately as Gorodish caressed her hair and face, touching her gently until her breathing became more regular.

Gorodish drove on, the Peugeot flying through the night. He smoked several cigarettes, trying to rid his mind of the ugly images that almost overcame his self-control, slowing down several times as his eyes became blinded by tears. The road blurred before him. One day someone would find Alcan's body underneath the oak tree. Gorodish felt as if he were moving through a dream.

He turned to look at Alba asleep in the backseat. The hours seemed to stretch interminably, the road growing longer as he drove. It seemed to him that they would never reach home.

It was almost two in the morning when Gorodish drove past the giant cedar tree and up to the house. New flowers were in bloom and the climbing roses exhaled a sweet scent. Careful not to wake Alba, he lifted her in his arms, opened the front door and crossed the dusty living room, glancing at the old piano before carrying Alba up the stairs and placing her on her bed. Gorodish opened the windows and looked out into the night, seeing the darker mass of the cedar tree silhouetted against the midnight-blue sky. Night odors seeped into the room. Gorodish lit a bedside lamp. Its dim light painted shadows on the wall and the room glowed pink as if illuminated by sunset.

Alba opened her eyes. Her vision began to clear and a veil of blood slowly dissipated as a myriad of ideas, impressions and images raced through her mind. There was a beautiful

125

face, a sweet face, bending over her. And a warm hand. And beyond the face a large tree standing silhouetted against the dark blue of the sky. She knew that tree. She was not dead. She knew that face and those dark eyes and that mouth. The house was silent and there was a good, familiar odor. The man bending over her was speaking, his voice deep and sweet as he repeated a name: Alba, Alba, Alba. There were shreds of confusion in her mind and she looked out at the tree again, then up at the face, hearing the word more clearly now. It was she: her name was Alba. She saw the cedar tree and she was in Gorodish's house and it was over. Charley and the others were dead and she was free, she was home, and the face bending over her was that of Gorodish.

He saw life come back into her eyes, saw the beginning of understanding, saw her tears, the blue of her eyes blurring. Then he heard her murmur, "Serge. . . ."

She raised herself up on one elbow and stared at him intently, with more passion than he had ever seen in a human gaze. Alba threw herself into his arms, straining against him, her delicate hands caressing him feverishly as she began to speak. She said the same word over and over again, ever louder, her voice filled with an elation that seemed to be devouring her very being. Joy took possession of them, shaking them to the core of their souls as they held each other tightly, passionately.

Sunrise touched the massive cedar tree, illuminating its height, its breadth, its beauty.

ABOUT THE AUTHOR

Who is "Delacorta"? That was the question that occupied Parisian literary circles upon the publication of *Diva* in France. After a year of speculation and mystery, the truth came out: Delacorta is the pen name of Daniel Odier, a young Swiss novelist and screenwriter about whom Anaïs Nin once wrote, "He is an outstanding writer and a dazzling poet."

Born in Geneva in 1945, Daniel Odier studied painting in Rome, received his university degree in Paris and worked as a music critic for a leading Swiss newspaper before taking off for a tour of Asia which resulted in a book on Taoism. His first book, *The Job: Interviews with William Burroughs*, was published in the United States in 1969. Since then he has published seven novels in France under his real name, two of which have become the basis for motion pictures by director Alain Tanner, and *Broken Dreams*, which will be made by director John Boorman. As Delacorta, he has written four books, *Diva, Nana, Luna* and *Lola;* the last has been made into a movie by French national television.

Mr. Odier now teaches at the University of Tulsa in Oklahoma, where he resides with his wife, the violinist Nell Gotkovsky.

127